ELISE STANKUS

if we fall

in the forest

Elise Stankus

Library of Congress Number: TXu-2-266-628

First paperback edition August 2021.

Edited by Elise Stankus, Janet Stankus, Alicia Ribeiro
Cover art by Daniel Mulcahy
Illustrations by Daniel Mulcahy
Layout by Elise Stankus

Printed by Blurb in the USA.

blurb.com

To My Fam...
and the Class of ...

"If a tree falls in the forest, and no one is
around to hear it,
does it even make a sound?"

- George Berkeley

ELISE STANKUS

part 1: summer

"Do I dare
Disturb the universe?
In a minute there is time
For decisions and revisions which a minute will
reverse"

- T.S. Eliot

ELISE STANKUS

01. parallels

ON APRIL 15, 1957, American physicist Hugh Everett first proposed his theory of parallel universes. Coincidentally, this was also the date, almost half a century later, that my father first announced that my twin sister Rosemary and I would be attending different high schools in the fall.

Up to that moment, Rosemary and I could've been parallel versions of the same person. We were always side by side, doing the same things, but we could never have lived the same life.

Rosemary likes people, and music, and stories, while I prefer reading doctoral theses on abstract physics concepts and math. Rosemary is outgoing, while my dad likes to say that I spend too much time in my head. I don't believe this is correct, since it is physically impossible to leave the confines of one's own head, but it makes Rosemary laugh, so I keep my thoughts to myself.

The idea of the multiverse, as proposed by Everett, states that countless universes exist in the same physical space, separated by the choices that our parallel selves make in each parallel reality. Each time a decision is made, the universe splits in two, allowing for infinite copies of the same person to exist simultaneously in his or her own version of reality.

From this, I concluded, everything on earth can be traced back to one decision that a specific person made at a specific time.

So everything that ever happened to me, everything I do, and everything I will do is the direct result of a choice either made by me or someone else at some time in the past, causing another branch to grow on the Universe Tree, which is how I like to think about it. Each time the universe splits into two different realities, one branch of the tree splits off from another, while every branch on the tree continues to grow all at the same time.

Sometimes I wonder whose choice gave rise to Rosemary and me, or whether we are truly parallel versions of the same person. I wonder whose choice determined my lack of hearing, and Rosemary's sense of music that I will never understand. And why we had to leave our comfortable homeschooled lives and go alone into the great unknown of high school.

On the morning of April 15, I was jolted awake by a dream, the details of which I promptly forgot. A glance at the clock told me it was already rather late, even for a Saturday morning. I opened my bedroom door and came face to face with my sister, whose bedroom was directly across from mine. Rosemary bounced out into the living room, already prepared for the day, while I lumbered behind, still half asleep. The two of us had just begun to fix breakfast when Dad walked into the kitchen, waving hello.

Can I see you girls in the living room when you're done eating?

I nodded, and Rosemary said something out loud that I couldn't make out.

Rosemary set her bagel down, and signed slowly to me. *I think something's up.*

Why? I replied.

3

Did you see how he didn't meet our eyes? He's nervous.

I shrugged. I was not good at reading people, even Dad and Rosemary. People were not as easy to decipher as words, or stories, or math problems. There was no index for a person, or a table of contents. I preferred reading other things.

We ate without signing, mostly because signing is difficult while eating, even for people who have been doing it their whole lives, like Rosemary and me. After we finished, Rosie began chatting, her hands flying as she told me about a million things at once. Although Rosie signed to me every day, arguably too often, this time something tugged at the back of my mind. A vague memory peeked its head out from the depths, and suddenly I was five years old again.

Rosemary and I were on a playground at the park on a street neighboring ours. The jungle gym was crawling with kids of all ages, all shapes and sizes. I was on one of the tallest slides, the one that was notorious in our neighborhood for scaring even the bravest kids. I had just made it to the top when I decided I didn't want to go down. I turned around, clumsily signing to Rosemary that I'd meet her at the bottom, in my broken five-year old signing. The boy behind Rosie and me was big, and when he saw me turning around, he laughed, and shoved me with one chubby hand that was as big as my head. Rosemary shoved him back, and began signing to him in angry bursts. The boy, obviously understanding nothing, pushed her, and before I knew what was going on, they were screaming at each other. The poor kids behind us had to back down the ladder to allow Dad to clamber up the slide and take us down. That was only one instance of many.

Rosemary would begin signing to strangers in supermarkets and parks, not realizing that it was something that most people could not do. I think that those were the first times Rosemary began to see that I was different.

After breakfast, we hesitantly crept into the living room, where Dad was drinking his coffee, his nose buried in the newspaper. We sat down on the couch, Rosemary plopping down on the corner seat closest to the window, and me sitting on the end seat, in the very middle of the cushion, below the lamp that looked like a marshmallow, so that a picture taken of me would be symmetrical.

It took a moment for Dad to realize we were there, even with Rosemary's flop on the couch.

When Dad read the newspaper, he read it cover-to-cover, even the stories about things that "no one wanted or needed to know," a phrase we heard most mornings. When he finally realized he wasn't alone, he set down the half-finished paper and took a long drink of coffee.

He spoke out loud as he signed. *Hey, girls. So. . .I wanted to talk to you about something.*

Rosemary shot me a look, and I watched Dad, slightly annoyed to see Rosie's imaginative fancies show up so early. She was always on a mission, or so she thought. Clearly, she read too many stories.

I've been thinking. Well, I'm not sure how to say this, to be perfectly honest. He paused. *I was recently made head of the history department at the university.*

Rosemary tilted her head. *Congratulations!*

Dad smiled. *Thank you. So I'll have to be at the university more. They're moving me to a full-time position again.*

Wait. I was confused. *How can you teach us, if you're at the university all day?*

Well. Dad stared at the floor as he leaned forward on the sofa. He took a deep breath, and his signing slowed, became more deliberate. *I thought, maybe, you two might want to think about going to a traditional school.*

Rosemary's hands flew. *I knew it! You're sending us to school!*

He smiled. *Only if you're okay with it. But your mom never wanted you to be homeschooled forever, you know.*

Wait. I signed. *Real school? With other kids?*

He nodded. *That's the idea.*

I stared straight ahead, so I could think. I had always hated change.

Dad went on, but Rosemary interrupted him before he could get very far. *What school?*

He paused. *That's - well, that's the thing. I've been looking at a few, but I think that's ultimately up to you.*

I straightened up in my seat. That seemed like an awful lot of responsibility. *What schools?*

He nodded. *Well. Remember where your mom went?*

Rosie's eyes widened. *Do you think I'd get in?* St. Michael's Preparatory School was a pretty prestigious private school whose students wore argyle sweaters and read poetry and got accepted into big universities.

He smiled a little, as though surprised by how well this conversation was going. *Worth a shot, right?*

Rosie closed her eyes. *Can you imagine? The uniform, the stone buildings. . .It would be wonderful, wouldn't it, Audrey?*

Dad nodded, and looked at me. *Audrey, you've been quiet.*

I was always quiet, but I knew that this was Dad's codified way of asking me what I was thinking. I shrugged. *I don't know,* I said.

His smile shrank a little. *Well. Audrey, I was wondering. I was looking at Ashton Heights High School. It has a really great STEM program, and there are better. . .accomodations than at St. Mike's. And I think you'd really love it there. So what do you think?*

I thought of the universe splitting in two as I thought about the choice in front of me. I thought of myself splitting in two along with it. *I don't know,* I signed truthfully, not meeting their eyes. So there was a version of me who continued to be homeschooled, and another version who went on to high school, which I'd heard was hard enough without any major life changes added to the mix. St. Michael's was a music school, with an auditorium that could seat a small city, which, of course, was not very appealing to me. But public school was daunting.

I know it's a lot, Dad went on. *You've got time to decide.*

I considered pointing out that there wasn't really time to decide, because the universe was splitting as we spoke, but some things are better left unsaid.

I thought about what he'd said. Accommodations. A long, heavy, cumbersome word. A word I had seen many times. It was one of only a few words that distinguished me from my sister. And I was smarter than Rosemary. I had read more, but she was a quicker learner. We had always learned together, worked together.

I hated the fact that I might have been holding her back, but it was probably true. Of course, I always helped her with math and science, which she had trouble with, but even I knew that she shouldn't be communicating in sign language for the rest of her life. I think my mother knew that. Rosie's signing was always somehow livelier than mine. You could tell from her signing that she could hear and speak. Her hand movements were graceful and exaggerated, almost birdlike. She understood language in a way I probably never would.

Later, when I was in my room, I saw the door hesitantly open, and Rosemary's face peeped in the doorway. *Can I come in?*

I nodded. She came in, stepping around the seven books I had splayed out on the floor, and sat down on my bed. *Hi,* she signed.

I waved.

So what do you think of all this? she asked, waving her arms to illustrate *all this* and nearly knocking over my purple lava lamp.

I thought of the millions of future possibilities that depended on my answer to her question. *How on earth will you pass math class without me?* I signed.

She laughed. *Hey, you'd better still help me with homework!* Her face got more serious. *I kind of can't believe it. I mean, there are like five hundred kids at St. Mike's Prep! I don't even know that many people!*

You'll be amazing, Rosie. I bet they have a nice music program or something. Rosemary was interested in everything, but she had always been particularly fascinated by creative pursuits.

I know. You gonna be okay with this?

I swallowed hard, but forced a smile. *Who, me?*

She grinned. *You'll probably be smarter than all the teachers, anyway.* She paused, looking a little sheepish. *Hey, can you explain quadratics to me again?*

I still don't get it. She laughed a little.

I've literally explained that to you four times already! I rolled my eyes, but I was smiling.

Oh, be quiet! She laughed as she slid off the bed, giving me a little sideways hug. *You're the best. I'll be back.*

She left to find her textbook, which she'd somehow misplaced again, and I was left alone for a few more moments. I straightened my bedspread, which Rosemary had scrunched up, and sat back down on the floor. I closed my physics textbook, but I couldn't stop thinking about my other selves, the parallel ones, who I would never know, but who were just as much Audrey Jean Cooper as I was. Even when Rosemary came back and plopped on the floor next to me, I couldn't get them out of my head, all the Audreys I could've been but wasn't.

Similar to the theory of parallel realities is the concept of parallel lines. Somewhat less abstract, parallel lines are lines with the same slope, in other words, lines that go on forever without crossing. I think that until April 15, Rosemary and I were parallel lines. We never crossed but nevertheless, my life was her life.

The summer before we started high school,

our paths began to drift farther apart. The cool thing about lines, though, is that the farther apart they grow on one end, they are bound to cross when you look in the opposite direction. For a moment in time, all the parallel versions of those lines are exactly the same.

02. names

BEFORE MY SISTER AND I WERE BORN, my parents didn't have any idea what they would name us. My mother, the poet, firmly believed that she couldn't name her daughters until she had met them. My father wanted to plan and pick names for us months in advance, but my mother insisted that they must not give us names that didn't suit us. As the story goes, we were named according to what we "looked like." When Audrey emerged, with me following a half hour later, my mother took one look at us, side by side in the little hospital bassinet, and declared us Audrey Jean and Rosemary Lane. Half-rhymes, like an Emily Dickinson poem.

I've always loved my name. It comes from

Latin, and translates to "dew of the sea." My mother, who lived and breathed poetry, used to call me that. When I was little, I was always confused. Dew-of-the-sea made no sense. Dew was made of water. The sea was made of water. Why did it matter where the water came from? I asked Mommy once, after a game of hide-and-seek with her and Audrey, during which she would call out, "Dewey! Where are you?"

Audrey's name means "Noble Strength," but oddly, I can't remember Mommy ever calling her that. Maybe she didn't need the reminder of who she was.

On this particular day, I was behind the curtains in the dining room, peeking out from behind the folds to watch Mommy. Her sign language was always a little clumsy and I tried not to laugh as she almost knocked over a lamp with an exaggerated hand movement. Audrey had disappeared, something she was quite good at, and was eventually discovered in the back of a closet in the basement.

After the game, which Audrey won (as usual), I climbed up on Mommy's lap and asked her, out loud, why she named me Dew-of-the-Sea. After I presented my four-year-old view of the situation, she laughed, and went into her "poetry mood," as Audrey and I liked to call it.

"Well," she said, looking out into nothingness, a habit that Audrey evidently inherited from her, "dew is not just any water. It's like glitter on the grass, or glaze on a donut." When she saw that I still didn't understand, she changed her analogy. "Think about the forest, Rosie. All the trees look the same at first glance, right? They're all trees." I nodded. "But only really special trees can turn into violins. Do you understand that?" I nodded again. "It's like that with the dew. The ocean is full of water, but the dew is different."

Seven years later, our mother died in a car crash. It shook my world like nothing ever had or ever would. She was on her way to a poetry reading when she was rear-ended by a dump truck. She was going to read her poems at a fundraiser for the Emily Dickinson Foundation. Her favorite poet.

The thing I remember most clearly about the day my mom died was Audrey's reaction, oddly enough. My dad came home from work with the news, and I remember wondering later how he could possibly have borne the car ride from work to our house, knowing he would have to deliver it. I hadn't previously realized that this was something that happened outside the movies, but when Dad told me, signing as he spoke for Audrey, I literally collapsed. I fell on my mom's favorite green carpet that we all hated, and just fell apart. My dad crouched down with me, and cried. It was the first and only time I'd ever seen him cry.

When I looked up, all I could see was Audrey's face. She sat on the couch, her hands folded, staring straight ahead of her with a blank look on her face. I was slightly horrified that she was showing no signs of distress, as though her entire world hadn't just collapsed. I thought at first she hadn't been watching when Dad signed to her, or that she hadn't processed the information. My face must've betrayed some level of anger, because Dad glanced Audrey's way, then back at me. He looked down for a moment, at the hideous carpet, then back up at me. "Let it be." he whispered. At first, I thought he was referencing the Beatles hit, which had always been Mom's favorite song. This only made me cry harder, but I later realized that this was his way of telling me to leave Audrey alone. She had her own way of doing things, even if we didn't always understand them.

I know that Audrey thinks that the first time I noticed her differences was the day on the playground when I started frantically signing to the bewildered children around me, but the day Mom died was the first day I realized how vast those differences were.

Even so, I had followed Audrey everywhere for most of my life. She was my hero, although she had done nothing spectacular to earn that title. She didn't need to.

I didn't have many close friends, but that didn't bother me. I liked being around people, but not necessarily interacting with them. The day Dad told us we'd be going to school, then, was a bit of a shock. My mother had always loved our connection, and even if she had started us in homeschool because of Audrey, I always thought she continued it so long because of me. So it was kind of a surprise when Dad said that Mom never wanted us to be homeschooled forever.

After we'd had our little family meeting, Audrey and I went to our rooms to think. My sister thinks best when she has math on her mind, but I think best with music.

I switched on my record player and slid in my mom's old record of *Let It Be*, turning the volume way down. I always felt a little bad listening to music because it was the one thing I couldn't share with Audrey, but in a way, that was also the reason I loved it so much.

My sister had known a lot of labels in her life. *Obsessive. Autistic. Deaf girl.* Even though she can't hear the whispers, I think she knows. Although I've always felt that the comments cut much deeper into me than her.

After a few songs, I went into her room. In our house, we didn't knock on doors. We signed as we spoke, even when it was just me and Dad. Maybe it was out of habit, or maybe it was because we were so afraid of hurting Audrey.

When I slipped into her room, I saw her sitting cross-legged on the floor of her pristine room, with high-school level textbooks opened in front of her, displaying glimpses of formulas and symbols that looked like a foreign language to me.

It surprised me again how little the news of the school change seemed to disturb her world. She seemed her usual quiet self, but I knew how hard she could be to read, even to Dad and me.

We signed a little to each other about school, and when she signed that she hoped my new school had a good music program, I was surprised. I had always tried to keep that part of me away from her. I hadn't realized that she knew how important that was to me.

A few weeks later, in the chaotic midst of high school applications and interviews, I announced to my dad that I wanted to play the violin. I had been thinking about what Audrey had said. She picked up on more than I gave her credit for. And of course, my mother's words were in my mind as they always were, telling me about the glittery dew on the grass, the special trees that were destined to be violins.

My dad didn't seem surprised. "That sounds like a great idea, Rosie," he said thoughtfully. "It'll probably be a good way to make friends, too."

So, towards the end of eighth grade, I first picked up a violin. I liked the feel of it, the weight of the wood in my hands, and I enjoyed picturing the tree that it had once been. My violin teacher, a distant acquaintance of my father's, was named Miss Strayer, which I thought sounded very musical.

I was a little nervous when Dad dropped me off on the day of my first lesson at Miss Strayer's house, a little row home close to my new school, which we drove by on the way. St. Michael's Preparatory School was bigger than I remembered, with big stone towers, almost like a castle. Dad had taught Miss Strayer in college, so I knew that technically she wasn't a complete stranger, but I had never met her. Since this was my first solo extracurricular, I was a little uneasy, but I held my violin case in front of me and stepped up to the front stoop with confidence.

There were little stained-glass windows all around the natural wooden door, so that you could peek in, but everything inside was washed in color and a little hazy, like the windows in church.

Miss Strayer opened the door, and I saw that much of her house was washed in color anyway, stained glass windows or not. The sun shone down on the dark hardwood floor, the colored panes sending shoots of light dancing across the floor like a kaleidoscope.

"Hi," I said, remembering at the last second that I didn't have to sign as I spoke.

"Hi, Rosemary!" she exclaimed. "I'm Miss Strayer. Come on in."

She ushered me in the door, and I saw that her house was a bit cluttered, like my bedroom, with wall hangings of all shapes and colors nearly covering the walls. I liked it instantly.

"Please forgive the clutter," she said. "I'm in

the middle of spring cleaning. The music room is this way."

I considered pointing out that it was almost July, and that she was out of time for spring cleaning, but I restrained myself, following her through a narrow hallway filled with mirrors and lots of different colored light fixtures.

We stopped in a room about halfway down the hallway, with all sorts of musical instruments strewn across the room. A baby grand piano sat in the corner, its glossy black table top covered with violin bows, guitar picks, and even a saxophone. Sheer curtains patterned with music notes framed a big picture window looking out over what appeared to be a golf course.

"So," Miss Strayer said with a smile as she sat down in an easy chair that she apparently employed as a piano bench, "I hear that you'll be attending St. Mike's in the fall. Are you excited?"

I shrugged. "Yeah. I'm a little nervous, too. Did you know I'm homeschooled?"

"I did. Your dad told me. He also told me your sister's going somewhere else."

I nodded.

"I'm a twin, too." she said. "I have a twin brother, and we never got along all that well, to be honest." She chuckled a little, shaking her head so that the colored beads in her braids clicked together, almost like a wind chime. "But when we went to college, I hardly saw him. That was pretty hard." She looked up at the ceiling thoughtfully, for a moment reminding me of Audrey. Her face hardened unexpectedly, but after a moment she seemed to come back down from her thoughts and back to me. She glanced down at her wrist, apparently expecting to find a watch there. Finding none, she looked up at the wall, where a little rectangular clock hung, its functional drabness juxtaposed against the chaos of the rest of the room. "Anyway. I don't expect that you came here to hear about my life, eventful as it is. Let's see that violin!"

I gingerly took it out of its case, as she dug around under her piano and pulled out a weathered violin-shaped case. She looked thoughtfully at me for a moment. "See, you've already got the basics down. Now, hold your instrument like you mean it!"

She taught me the basics of how to rosin the bow, how to hold it, and how to pluck the strings, all things that a quick search through the music section of the public library had already taught me. However, Miss Strayer's unique brand of enthusiasm and musical knowledge gave me much more skill than the whole of the library's music section could have.

She showed me how to play some simple tunes, and before we knew it, the hour was up. I left her colorful lair a lot more confident than when I'd walked in. I walked out into the sunshine wielding my violin case with a new sense of purpose.

When I arrived home, I found Audrey just as I had left her - in the middle of a pile of textbooks. *Hey, Aud*, I signed.

How was it? She signed without looking up from what she was scribbling in a thick notebook.

Fine. Good. It was good. For some reason I couldn't quite identify, I wanted to keep Miss Strayer's wonderful, crazy chaos to myself. It was too intricate a beauty to explain.

I turned to go, but saw Audrey signing out of the corner of my eye. I spun around. *You should keep doing it*, she said. *I bet you're really good at it.*

Thanks. Perplexed, I turned and walked out. Audrey wasn't good with people, but sometimes, I thought, she knew me better than I did.

I came out into the living room, where Dad was watching a soccer match on television. "Hey," he said. "Wanna do somethin'? Watch a movie?"

I nodded. I liked change, but this much change could be overwhelming. Dad hadn't asked for specific details about the lesson, but I knew he didn't need them. The great thing about Dad was that he never asked us to explain ourselves. He knew that we would tell when we were ready.

I sat down on the couch, suddenly realizing how tired I was, and smiled as Dad pulled out a DVD and slid it in the player. I hadn't realized how loud my life had gotten. The quiet felt nice.

After the movie, we all sat down for dinner. Dad had gotten takeout Chinese as a surprise, and we sat in relative silence for a while while we ate. Halfway through his lo mein, Dad turned and pointed a chopstick at Audrey, before setting it down so he could talk to her.

So, Audie, he signed, using the nickname that no one had called Audrey in years, *Rosie's playing the violin now. Do you want to start something new? Math team, maybe? Or an art class? Or maybe there's a science fair you could do?*

I like the things I do now, she said. She fiddled with her hands a little before continuing. *I'm in eighth grade, Dad. I can pick my own hobbies.*

He tilted his head to the side. I was surprised, too. I think that Dad thought that if one of us would speak to him like that, it would be me. He nodded, trying to conceal his surprise, and we finished the meal in silence.

After dinner and homework, I went into Audrey's room again. She was reading this time, an astrophysics book that would have gone way over my head. I waved. *Hi, Aud.*

She didn't look up. She was usually pretty good at detecting sign language from across a room. My sister had perfect vision, some cruel trick of the universe to compensate for the other cards she was dealt, I supposed. But today, she didn't seem to notice me. I considered going over and tapping her shoulder, but I knew how jumpy she was. If she was so tired she couldn't see me, or if she just wanted to read, I would just let her be. Or maybe she didn't want to talk to me. In the end, I left without saying anything.

I wasn't quite sure what I would've said, anyway.

03. music (vibraTions)

I THINK THE DAY Rosemary and I really started to go our own ways was the day she started playing the violin. I'd always felt like she'd be a great musician, as my mother had been. I understood her hesitation, though. I know I can be a burden sometimes. And the dynamic in our house was changing. The violin began to take up more and more of my sister's time. Rosie began to spend hours and hours alone, which I almost didn't notice. Instead of spending time with me, either reading quietly in my room while I studied, or watching TV, or just simply sitting together, she would spend a half hour practicing one day, forty minutes the next, and so on, until it was pushing four hours. I have always preferred being alone, but I didn't realize how dependent I was on my sister's visits.

A few weeks after Rosemary started practicing all the time, she came into my room while I was reading. She waved, and I realized she was holding her violin. *Do you mind if I practice here?* she asked. *I'm tired of being alone all the time.*

I shrugged, but I was surprised. I didn't know if Rosie knew how much her practicing had changed my daily routine. Did she want to hang out with me, or not? I went back to my book, until she touched the bow to the string. I felt a peculiar buzzing in my head, and my head snapped up. Rosie's eyes widened, a puzzled look on her face. I'm sure I looked puzzled, too.

Again, I signed. She drew the bow across the lowest string, and I closed my eyes. It was as though the string was vibrating directly inside my brain. Suddenly, the vibration became lighter, and I opened my eyes. Rosie had moved on to the next string.

What is it? She asked.

I closed my eyes again, still feeling the vibrations. *I can feel it.*

You can what?

I stood up, walked over to her, and put my hand on the smooth wood of the instrument. It was lighter than I expected, and delicate. *Play.*

She played a series of notes this time, the vibrations becoming harsher and then softer as she went from note to note.

Rosie set the violin down, the corner of her mouth turning up in a half-smile. *What does it feel like?*

I thought about it. It wasn't like anything I'd ever experienced before. *It feels like. . .like what I thought sound would feel like,* I signed slowly, hoping that she would know what I meant. Her puzzled expression showed that she did not. I took the violin from her and holding it in front of me, I dragged the bow across a string. *You try.*

I took her hand in mine and pressed it to the back of the instrument, like I had done, and dragged the bow across again. *Do you feel it?*

A little. She still looked confused, and shook her head. *No, not really.* She tilted her head to the side. *It's like you have a superpower, Aud.*

I shrugged. *Can you play some more?*

I went back to my chair, and sat down with my book, feeling the music course through my head. It wasn't the chaotic buzzing that I sometimes felt when I was in a room with a lot of people talking at the same time, but more *organized*, somehow.

I had always thought of music as a divider of sorts. Something that stood between me and everyone else. But perhaps it didn't have to be that way.

A few weeks later, in mid-July, I went for a tour of my new school. It was finally warming up, and I was rather reluctant to spend a warm day of summer vacation at school. Ashton Heights High School was one of the biggest buildings I'd ever been in, with long hallways where people looked like ants at the other end of them. The walls were made of huge whitewashed cinder blocks, and the floor was made of checkered tiles that made me feel like a chess pawn. The edge of the board felt like a long way from where I stood.

My tour guide's name was Annika, a tall, blond sophomore at Ashton Heights, with big round glasses that made her look intelligently goofy. She signed slowly, as though she hadn't been doing it for very long, about the teachers' extensive training in ASL as part of some inclusivity program, the details of which I neither understood nor wanted to, for that matter. I hoped with all I had that the teachers' training was more extensive than Annika's had been.

She showed me most of the rooms where I would have my classes, which looked, more or less, like what I expected public school classrooms to look like. The English classroom was plastered with colored posters and literary magazines. I internally shuddered at the explosion of colors and shapes spilling out of the room. I had never enjoyed English class, for the same reason I hated parties. There was too much happening at once in a storybook, as well as at a party. I would rather have my attention focused on a particular thing before moving on to another. Unfortunately, the state Department of Education required at least two foundation English courses. (I had read up on the requirements a few days prior.)

A few of the teachers were in their classrooms, and they signed to me with an air of vague politeness, explaining to me the details of their respective programs. I signed *hello*, and nodded at the correct times throughout the conversations, but for the most part avoided eye contact. There were more people than I was used to being around, and it was making me a little nervous, even though Dad was in the building, taking a different tour. Eventually, we moved onto the cafeteria, which was much bigger than I expected, with lights dimmed and walls garishly painted in the school's colors, purple and gold.

It was odd, being in this huge building full of strangers. Although I was fourteen, circumstances had not allowed for me to go on a whole lot of solo outings into the wider world. Even if they had been offered, I would not have chosen to go.

The last classroom that Annika showed me was the music room. She looked rather uncomfortable as she explained the basics of the school's music program, which I assumed was the general procedure for visiting students. I understood her discomfort. Despite the fact that showing me the music room was probably unnecessary, I hadn't really said anything to her, which I knew made some people uncomfortable, though it was my preferred state.

Soon enough, we reunited with Dad and his tour guide, and we met with the principal to discuss the administrative side of things. I was tired by then, and just wanted to go home and read.

On the way home, in Dad's minivan, Rosemary and Dad asked me question after question about the day, and I marveled at the world's ability to sustain such hectic lives.

When we got home, Rosie retreated to the safety of her violin, and I to my books. If I closed my eyes and stood very still, I could feel the instrument singing through the walls.

04. homeschOol

ONE SUNDAY, early in the summer, the three of us sat in the third pew from the front at Our Lady of the Rosary Church, just like every Sunday morning. And just like every week, I tried to pay attention, but my mind wandered like the little kid in the pew in front of us, whose mother had to chase him down the center aisle when he ventured too far.

I always felt closest to my mom when we were in church. She had always loved it, and sat with a look of such joy on her face that I wondered if we were seeing the same thing. I enjoyed the hymns, and listened as best as I could to the readings, but I had never quite grasped my mom's unbridled enthusiasm. I closed my eyes as the priest gave the final blessing, and tried my best to pay attention. I pictured my mom in the seat next to me, and smiled.

Some people hear the word "homeschooled" and think of overprotective parents and strict Catholic rules. My mother always had a dream, I think, a vision of herself as a homesteading, homeschooling, upstanding Catholic mother, tending her garden, writing her poetry, and hosting Bible studies. She was firm in her belief, firm in every belief she ever had.

She always encouraged us to branch out, though Audrey and I were content with each other's company most of the time. It was funny how sometimes our mother would praise us for sticking together, for sticking up for one another and sticking up for ourselves, and other times she commended us on our ability to branch out and be different people. This might seem like she praised us no matter what we did, which was not true. That was just the way she was.

Occasionally, I would go out with friends, but the rarity of those outings was due to the fact that if I was being honest, I did not enjoy them. I loved hanging out with people, but for some reason I always felt out of place among those "friends" with whom I had very little in common, either the children of my parents' friends, or acquaintances from church, where I attended a play group for most of my childhood. That is, until Mom died. I used to have a lot of "friends," back when Mom would take us places.

Dad says that Mommy had always wanted to homeschool her kids. When Audrey and I were younger, she used to join us in whatever craft or art project we were working on, jamming her fingers into the tiny safety scissors she had picked out for us. When we got a little older, we often found her studying our math textbooks with a sheepish look on her face, preparing to teach us how to solve problems she didn't know how to solve herself. Mom was an English major, and always told us that she never understood the purpose of mathematics, but if the state required her to teach it, then she'd try her best, especially as Audrey enjoyed it so much.

Even so, I think she had a secret hope that Audrey would come to love poetry, the thing my mother loved so much. She tried to encourage us to read all sorts of things, without being imposing. I loved it, but I think I came by that naturally. She tried to help me enjoy math, although her attempts were somewhat futile, considering she did not enjoy it herself. Sometimes it seemed like she had made it her personal mission to inspire in my sister some sort of creative literary spark, but my sister stuck to her mathematics and I to my novels. I think maybe this was another dream she never quite reached.

One of my happiest memories of my mom was when she was trying to teach us the concept of fractions one day in fourth grade, an attempt to make math more fun, as I had already shown a vague dislike. Instead of using the hypothetical situation of a pizza being cut into any number of slices, Mom made an actual homemade pizza, teaching us about yeast risen dough and how to throw the pizza dough in the air to flatten it into a disk. Unfortunately, she threw it too high, and it stuck to the ceiling. We stood in shock, mouths wide open for a long moment, before it peeled off the ceiling with a great sucking, slurping sound, and all three of us simultaneously lurched forward to catch it. We caught it, but tripped over each other in the process, landing in a tangled heap, covered in a sheet of sticky but fortunately unsoiled pizza dough. We sat and laughed for a while, before Dad walked in and stopped in his tracks, making us laugh even harder. In the end, we used the same dough to form our pizza, and once it was finished, Mom cut it into two pieces, then four, then eight, then sixteen, and so on. She brandished her pizza cutter like a sword, cutting the steaming pizza as delicately as though she was performing surgery. In the end, she was able to cut it into 1128 slices, all of different sizes and shapes but all similarly mutilated. Mom was also thoroughly covered in cheese and tomato sauce by the end of the procedure. Although we were practically dying of laughter at that point, Mom divided up the 1128 slices of pizza, which were rapidly congealing into a pinkish mush, into roughly three piles. Delighted with the rare opportunity to eat with our fingers, Audrey and I scooped up the messy glop and shoved it into our mouths while Mommy laughed and laughed and laughed.

Our curriculum changed drastically after she died. Dad had always been so busy teaching his college classes that he never really spent much time with us during school days, and so he had very little idea how to teach us. He was used to teaching material that we wouldn't be able to understand for years, to kids almost twice our age. On second thought, Audrey may have been able to understand it, but I definitely couldn't have.

Sometimes he would get frustrated with us for not understanding, as though he had forgotten we were middle schoolers and not the grad students he was accustomed to working with. I don't blame him, though. To be perfectly honest, I know that Audrey and I were tough students to have. Audrey has always had this habit of receding into her mind like a turtle into a shell, and it's hard to reach her there, even for me. As for me, even with Mom's engaging and slightly unconventional methods of teaching, I found myself distracted more times than not, and I knew Mom's patience grew thin at times.

So when Dad said he couldn't teach us much more, I knew that what he really meant was that he didn't have the patience or the time to teach us anymore. Even as our work became more independent as we advanced, teaching Audrey and I could be a challenge, even for a college professor.

Although I had friends who were in a traditional school, and had read plenty of books about the angst-filled days of high school, my orientation at St. Michael's Preparatory School came as kind of a shock. Upon walking in the door alone, since Dad had dropped me off on the way to

Audrey's school tour, I was greeted courteously - but not warmly - by someone I assumed to be the receptionist. A tall, well-groomed woman in a blazer, with sleek dark hair piled into a knot on the top of her head, she introduced herself as Mrs. Q. That seemed to me a wonderfully mysterious name, and I was instantly curious about her, despite her indifferent air. After introducing herself, she handed me a pamphlet containing small black text full of phrases like "award-winning administration" and "top-notch facilities" and "students of exceptional talent" alongside glossy photos of beautiful, uniformed students. My playful curiosity at Mrs. Q.'s name slowly dissipated as I skimmed the pamphlet, which seemed all too full of standards that I could never meet.

Mrs. Q. ushered me over to a leather couch in the lobby, which had brick walls and a high vaulted ceiling, with frosted windows overlooking the parking lot.

"Your tour guide will be here shortly," she said curtly. I nodded and smiled. "I'm sorry dear, what is your name?" she asked, her eyes softening slightly.

"Rosemary Cooper." Since I was a little uneasy, I signed out the words as I spoke, without thinking.

She watched my hands as they fluttered to spell out my name, but didn't comment on it.

"Ah, yes. Rosemary. That's my granddaughter's name, you know,"

I smiled politely, and nodded.

The inside of the building was very similar to the outside, with stone walls and high ceilings. It reminded me of pictures I'd once seen of a monastery. It was a very far cry from homeschool. It seemed to me a place of great adventure.

Despite the many benefits of learning at home, one of the drawbacks is just that: learning at home. The days learning with my mother's experimentations were the best of my life, but even the most adventurous homeschooler has to resign herself to some level of quietness. The homeschool days were quiet, not boring. But even so, I found myself looking for something new.

This was one of the reasons I was eager to begin attending a traditional school. I had never seen much of the world outside my town, and a part of me wanted the life of adventure I'd always read about in fantasy stories. I loved my sister, but didn't want to communicate solely in sign language for the rest of my life. I was terribly sorry that she had to.

And so I went into high school, so to speak, hungry for adventure. I was Samwise Gamgee searching for the elven kingdom, King Arthur looking for the Holy Grail. I was a deeply dramatic, intensely ambitious future high schooler in search of something - I just didn't know what I was looking for yet.

ELISE STANKUS

part 2. autumn

"I am struck by the fact that the more slowly trees grow at first, the sounder they are at the core, and I think that the same is true of human beings."

-Henry David Thoreau

ELISE STANKUS

05. firsT days

I'VE ALWAYS HATED FIRST DAYS. So many unfamiliar things, so many unknowns. Even the first days of a new homeschool year posed some threat to my peace of mind, though the curriculum often changed very little from year to year. But of course, this year was different.

After Dad insisted on taking our "first day of high school photos" under the maple tree in the backyard far too early in the morning, Rosemary and I boarded our respective buses. I had never had the occasion to board a school bus before, and was slightly taken aback by the dirt that seemed to be everywhere inside it, especially considering the clean atmosphere of the school. It had seeped into every nook and crevice, and after a while, I began to feel contaminated myself. We arrived, after many bumps that reminded me of an old wooden roller coaster, at the square brick building which was to be the setting of the next four years of my education.

Once the bus lurched to a stop, I hauled my overfilled backpack onto my shoulder and tried to mentally prepare myself for the day. I had hastily said goodbye to Rosemary, since Dad's photoshoot had given us less than enough time to get sufficiently ready for school, which was, of course, not the ideal way to start a school year. I wondered if Rosie had arrived at her big fancy private school yet.

I could see people talking as I stepped off the bus. There were more kids filing in the big double doors than I thought would fit in such a building. Someone shoved into me as I walked through the doors, and I almost stumbled, but caught myself on the doorway. I looked behind me, but there was such a jumble of kids behind me that I figured it was an accident. At least I hoped it was.

I had received my schedule in the mail a few weeks prior, and Annika the poorly-trained-tour-guide had managed to show me where my homeroom would be, so I had a vague idea of where to go. I went up a dimly lit staircase and found my way to the homeroom, a fairly small classroom on the third floor. A short, stocky middle-aged woman with hair in a messy bun greeted me at the doorway. *Hello, you must be Audrey*, she signed with bubbling enthusiasm.

I nodded.

My name is Mrs. Maddox. I'll be your homeroom teacher this year.

Hello. Mrs. Maddox looked ecstatic at making my acquaintance. I was familiar with this. When someone is not sure what to make of my lack of hearing, or of anyone who seems different in any way, they tend to assume that they are in some way inferior, and treat them the way they would treat a very young child.

Come right in. You can sit at any open desk.

I walked into the classroom, which was already about half full, plopped my black bookbag on the chessboard floor, and sat down at a desk in the back, closest to the window. The checkered pattern on the floor was made of wooden squares of varying darkness, just like my chessboard at home. My mother was the only person who could ever beat me at chess.

My chair sat on one of the darker wooden squares. I wondered which piece I would be in this game.

I looked down at my desk, which was covered in scratches and indecipherable carvings. Kids all around me were talking. When the bell rang, I got up and went straight to the next class, while my classmates stopped at their lockers to chat, to laugh, to eat, to get a book they forgot. It seemed that I was the only one on a straight course, determined to get in and out.

I walked through the rest of my classes in a bit of a fog. I understood all the academic material, even when I skipped to the end of the textbooks because I was bored.

It was interesting to be able to pick all my classes, rather than being assigned a particular curriculum, like I was used to. Although, my mom's enthusiasm and odd additions to our school day always made it plenty interesting.

In chess, the rook, or the castle, is the only piece that can only move in straight lines. It sits in the corner, safe behind all the pawns, and is often one of the last pieces to move. While everyone was gathering around the kings and queens, I did my best to stay in the corners, moving quickly through the day, in the straightest line possible. The only rook.

06. language

THE FUNNY THING about growing up with two languages is that at first, you don't realize they're any different. For most of my childhood, I regarded spoken English and signed English as the same thing, or at least two aspects of the same thing. I spoke as I signed and I signed as I spoke. I knew that I had to sign when addressing Audrey, but I didn't realize until I was five or six that the spoken words and the hand motions could be separated. They had always been connected in my mind, and still were.

Even when we're signing to each other, it often seems like Audrey and I speak two different languages. We move our hands and somehow we know what the other is trying to say. But movements can't convey everything. Languages are odd that way.

The previous summer, I had slaved over my schedule. I wanted to make sure I was taking the best, most fun classes, but the foreign language requirement had stumped me for the longest time. Maybe it was because language at my house took a different shape than it did elsewhere. Or maybe I was just being indecisive. Throughout my years of homeschool, I had never taken a language besides ASL, which didn't even count, because I was fluent by the time I was in second grade.

In the end, I decided on Latin, since it seemed easier, my mother had liked it, and because I could still hear her whispering "dew of the sea" to me as I fell asleep.

On the second day of school, a Thursday, I walked into last period Latin and heard the teacher, a late middle-aged woman with too much knowledge of philosophy, speaking in Latin. Only Latin.

Fern Reynolds, who I could already tell sat comfortably atop the metaphorical food chain of high school girls, raised her hand. "Are you aware we don't speak Latin?" she asked, her heart-shaped face a perfect imitation of innocence.

Mrs. Perez shot her a look as though Fern was nothing more than an annoying fly buzzing around her head, and continued to speak in a language that none of us understood. After a good 10 minutes of this, she switched to English. "If I were to speak like that every day, you would learn to speak perfect Latin," she said with an imperious air. "However, the school board requires that I follow the curriculum."

She cleared her throat. "This is a language class." While some boys in the back snickered, she went on. "Who knows what language was invented for?"

The room quieted down, as everyone sank deep in thought, or at least pretended to. One girl in the back raised her hand. "For historical records?" Mrs. Perez nodded. "Partially," she said.

A hand shot up in the front. "For the cavemen to write captions for their cave drawings," a boy said. His friends rolled their eyes.

"Hmm." said Mrs. Perez, deeply considering this response. "And the cavewomen. Interesting answer. Anyone else?"

"For poetry," came a quiet voice from the back.

"For stories."

"To put an end to awkward silences?"

An assortment of answers, all of varying levels of sarcasm, came from throughout the room.

Eventually, Mrs. Perez folded her hands in front of her floral skirt with a sigh. "For *communication*, ladies and gentlemen," she said. "Language was invented so that we can *communicate* with each other."

A murmur of *ahh* rippled across the class.

"Therefore," Mrs. Perez continued, "before we start our study of *language*, we must first learn about *communication*."

I could almost hear the eye rolls of students wanting an easy A, but I was kind of intrigued by this strange approach.

She went on, describing the human need for interpersonal communication, and I thought about language. I wondered who first had the idea to use sounds to communicate. I pictured a burly caveman scratching pictures on stone walls. Why was verbal language necessary when they could communicate through pictures? Why didn't they choose hand signals? Or music? I thought about Audrey's strange reaction to the playing of my violin. If deaf people could feel music in a way they could not experience speech, why wasn't music our primary form of communication?

I tuned back into class, where Mrs. Perez was still talking. "I cannot teach you basic human communication, but I want you to be on the lookout. In what ways do you communicate besides words? Is your communication different with, say, your parents, than with your classmates? How about your friends?'

The same boy who had spoken up before did so again. "Will this be on the test?"

Mrs. Perez looked him in the eye. "Yes. Not on any test I give you, but I promise, this information will serve you well." Mrs. Perez's eyes were intense.

About two-thirds of the students groaned at this comment. This was a much different approach to education that my mother's. My mother always taught material the most direct way she knew how. Granted, this often included poetic digressions and seemingly unrelated endeavors like the pizza incident. Mrs. Perez seemed a bit more confused about what subject she was teaching. Nevertheless, I kept thinking about it all day.

That afternoon, I had a violin lesson. I arrived a few minutes early, and Miss Strayer let me in with a big smile. The beads in her hair were different colors, red and orange and yellow and green. The colors of changing leaves. Despite her claim during my first lesson that she was in the middle of spring cleaning, her battle against the clutter still did not seem to be going well. Either that, or she was still in the middle of spring cleaning.

We played a violin duet, an adaptation of *Autumn*, one of the Four Seasons concertos by Vivaldi. Miss Strayer told me that she had arranged it herself, and I was curious. Miss Strayer was fluent in the language that I was just beginning to learn.

After we played through the arrangement a couple of times, she pulled a book off one of the wall-to-wall bookshelves in the music room. Most of the shelf space was not used for books, but this book was especially intriguing, a well-worn, leather-bound volume as thick as a Bible. Before I could get a glimpse of the title, she sat the book next to me with a great thump. It was open to a page titled Autumn. One side of the page was a sheet of music. The page was yellowed, and I squinted to make out the small print. It read *Autumn, Vivaldi* and below the title was a poem. I looked up quizzically at Miss Strayer. "A poem?"

She nodded. "Vivaldi wrote poems to accompany each of the Four Seasons, each stanza corresponding to a movement of the concerto."

"Huh." I sat down to read it.

I. *Allegro--*
The peasants celebrate with dance and song,
The joy of a rich harvest.
And, full of Bacchus's liquor,
They finish their celebration with sleep.

II. *Adagio molto--*
Each peasant ceases his dance and song.
The mild air gives pleasure,
And the season invites many
To enjoy a sweet slumber.

III. *Allegro--*
The hunters, at the break of dawn, go to the
            hunt.
With horns, guns, and dogs they are off,
The beast flees, and they follow its trail.
Already fearful and exhausted by the great
            noise,
Of guns and dogs, and wounded,
The exhausted beast tries to flee, but dies.

The first two stanzas were soft, and quiet, while the third rang with gunshots and the hunt. It was interesting, I thought, how music and words could convey such a similar meaning.

I said goodbye to Miss Strayer, and later, while doing the dishes, I hummed *Autumn*, looking out the window at the changing leaves and thinking about the poem. I remembered what Mrs. Perez had asked just hours earlier: *"In what ways do we communicate besides words?"* It seemed an odd way to open a class that focused, I expected, on words, but I was beginning to see what she meant.

07. trees

LAST PERIOD, I had biology, but I was already familiar with the information that the teacher was beginning to introduce. I had spent hours at home, curled over my books, reading about biology and chemistry and astrophysics. It was so fascinating to me to find out what things were made of, how they were made, why they were made. It was comforting to learn about something so cleanly cut, with no exceptions and no shortcuts.

I was tired. I was sick of signing to people. The school day hadn't been seven hours long yet, but it had been so full of new experiences that it seemed much longer. School days at home were generally quiet, while today had been big and loud.

My head vibrated like the violin every time I ventured into the hallway, the raised voices penetrating through my head, even though I couldn't hear them. In a way, it was more than a first day. It was a *first* first day, even more new than all the others.

I opened up my biology textbook, thick and heavy and dripping with information. I skipped to a random page towards the end, and began reading. "Mother Trees and Root Systems," a bold heading read. The passage was full of scientific terms and fascinating new ideas, and I drank it all in. The book explained how trees communicate to each other in the forest, a concept that was foreign to me. Wise old trees, known as mother trees, can communicate to trees up to seven miles away, solely through root systems and airborne chemicals. They can send distress signals to other trees when faced with danger, and can send water and sugars to seedlings too young to photosynthesize. I looked up, my eyes widening as my mind unpackaged this new information.

If trees could communicate and we didn't know for thousands of years, what else is happening on this planet that we haven't discovered yet? Could trees evolve so that they could communicate in other ways, perhaps with humans? And why? Why would a tree sacrifice its own nutrients to support another, a youngling that would grow up to be its rival? My mind swirled.

I thought about the universe splitting, and all the possibilities that existed all at the same time. Somewhere, sometime, there is a universe in which trees are valiantly fighting and sacrificing and going to battle. In another, they are silent loners, mindlessly competing for nutrients. In yet another, they were another thing entirely. But which was happening in our own universe? I didn't know.

I thought suddenly about the Schrodinger's Cat experiment. In the 1930s, an Austrian physicist working with Albert Einstein came up with the thought experiment that came to be known as Schrodinger's Cat. He devised a hypothetical situation in which a cat is placed in a box with a radioactive substance. The box is then sealed. There is an equal probability that the cat will be killed by the radioactive substance and that it will remain alive. Schrodinger's point was that until the box is opened, no one can say whether the cat is alive; while the box is closed, the cat is *both alive and dead* simultaneously. In other words, the reality of the living cat and the reality of the dead cat do not split until the box is opened. The universes can't separate until someone makes the decision to separate them.

I like this experiment because it explains the concept of parallel universes so clearly, even before Everett gave the theory a name. Each one of us is a cat in a box with a deadly substance in it. We are both dead and alive at the same time, deaf and hearing, asleep and awake. As long as you keep the box closed, you never have to face a bad outcome.

This seemed strangely relevant, I thought, as my mind turned over the new ideas I had just discovered. I had never been much of an outdoorsy person, although I grew up in a family of them. I liked nature because it was scientifically fascinating, while my sister loved it for its beauty and the inspiration she got from it. Or something like that.

I almost fell asleep on the car ride home from school, though it was not very long. Dad peppered me with questions, like *how was your day?* and *what did you do?* and *who did you sit with at lunch?* My hands moved slowly. *Good. Not much. Nobody.*

A few hours later, I sat in my room, bent over a few books but not really reading them. Dad had looked at me in the way that I knew meant *you're spending too much time alone.* And maybe I was. But that was the only way I knew how to be.

Rosemary said I spend too much time in my head. And she was probably right. But on days like this, it wasn't like locking myself in my room, or going outside to be alone. It felt more like being stuck. It wasn't even my mind wandering. It closed up, like my eyes, and then it was like sleeping.

08. orcHestra (adventure)

ON SEPTEMBER 3rd, the third day of school, I walked through the big double doors and was greeted by a bustling crowd in the main hallway. A sign above my head read CLUB SIGN UP. I made my way to a table, and hesitantly shoved my way into the crowd. The first table I came to had a big hand-painted sign advertising ORCHESTRA: ALL SKILL LEVELS WELCOME in blue block letters.

I thought of my violin, and then I thought of my mother telling me about the special trees that became instruments, and then I picked up my pencil and scrawled my name on the clipboard. I then walked through the halls with a sense of purpose. I had joined a club.

And so on the next day of school, I walked into the orchestra room, wielding my violin case like armor. I remembered Audrey's observation and figured I was probably experienced enough for an orchestra that had no tryouts. The room was big and spacious, with high ceilings and windows taller than me.

Students filed through the door, carrying a wide variety of instruments. I sat down near a couple of other violinists, none of whom I recognized. The orchestra conductor, a tall older man named Mr. Alden, stood up from the piano bench he had been sitting at, and waved at us with a conducting baton.

"Hello, musicians," he began in a voice that reminded me of the sound my sneakers made when I walked on the gravel footpaths at my favorite park. Mr. Alden looked towards the doorway with dismay as one last student scampered in the door, obviously well aware that she was late. I made a mental note to always be on time, or at least to try to be on time. I looked over. The newcomer was Fern Reynolds, the outspoken girl from Latin class. She surveyed the room and took the last available chair, which happened to be next to me. I smiled politely.

After Mr. Alden had introduced himself, he cleared his throat. "Now, let's get down to business." He passed out glossy black folders.

"These will be your folders for the year," he explained, "so take good care of them. Your music for this semester is inside. You may mark it up in whatever way you see fit, but keep in mind you must return the folders at the end of the year."

I opened the black plastic folder. Inside were two packets of sheet music. I took out the first, "Carol of the Bells for Strings," and opened up to the first page. Inside was the music I'd be playing in the winter concert, along with a piece of cream-colored paper, meticulously folded but still flat enough that it was undetectable when the packet was closed. The paper was very thin, and through the folds I could see the faint impression of pencil-scrawled letters.

I looked around the room, to see if anyone else was opening up a similar note. Everyone else seemed to be poring over their music, nothing more. I slipped the note into the pocket of my plaid uniform skirt, already wondering when I would have time to open it.

Audrey thinks I read too many fantasy novels, and she may be right, for as Mr. Alden explained the more boring aspects of orchestra, scheduling and so on, all I could think about was the note and all the adventures it could contain. Of course, it was entirely possible, even probable, that it was just a piece of paper someone lost, or a stupid note that kids had been passing and forgot in the folder.

After we were dismissed, armed with instruments and sheet music, I flew to my locker and tore open the paper. I counted the times I unfolded it. Nine. Someone had managed to fold this paper nine times. Someone, presumably, who wanted a bit of secrecy for their message. Or maybe someone who was bored and tried to see how many times they could fold a piece of paper. But who could say? And either way, why would they put it in a random music folder?

Once I undid the last fold, I smoothed out the many creases in the note, holding it against the door of my locker. There was a faint message inscribed on the paper in pencil. I squinted to read it.

September seven. Library. 3:00. The words were scrawled on a sheet of paper with a poem on it. It appeared to be taken from a textbook. I read the poem, grateful for my mother's poetry coaching.

"Sometimes when I watch trees sway,
From the window or the door.
I shall set forth for somewhere,
I shall make the reckless choice
Some day when they are in voice
And tossing so as to scare
The white clouds over them on.
I shall have less to say,
But I shall be gone."

The last line was underlined boldly. *I shall be gone.* It was a bit ominous, and I involuntarily shivered, wondering about the importance of that specific line. I stared at the poem for a long time, wondering what it could mean. Did it end up in my folder by accident? I hoped not.

It occurred to me again that the note could be nothing more than a joke, an attempt to humiliate me in front of my peers, but no one knew me very well anyway. Plus, this was just the type of adventure I had been longing for. Perhaps it was a treasure map or an invitation to the meeting of a secret organization that had accidentally fallen into my hands. But why would its writer place it in such a vulnerable spot as in a folder, without knowing who would end up with it? It was a mystery, for sure. One I was determined to solve, even though I was slightly unsure about pursuing it. Despite my misgivings, I made up my mind to be at the library at 3:00 on September 7th.

I arrived at the school library at 2:58. To my surprise, it was empty. I sat in a comfy chair in the corner, by a window, and waited. At 3:01, Fern Reynolds came spilling through the double doors. She stopped when she saw me. "Hi," she said hesitantly, evidently surprised to see me. I was just as surprised to see her. She surveyed the room and, finding no one else, sat down in an easy chair on the other side of the library. She walked like a princess, I thought. She moved as though she wore a crown on her head.

Was it possible she had gotten a note, too? Or could she have sent it? She clearly hadn't come for a book, although I wasn't surprised by that. She didn't seem like much of a reader. We waited a few minutes. I considered taking a book and reading, but if she had also gotten a note, I wanted her to know that I was in on it. If I started reading, it might look like that was all that I had come for. I wondered momentarily if I was overthinking the entire situation, but soon dismissed the thought.

We waited in silence, just the two of us. I

watched her out of the corner of my eye. Fern seemed like the kind of girl in books that you would want to stay away from. She was wearing a black sweater, a pink miniskirt and, I think, some makeup, an outfit right out of High School Musical. Her black hair sat in two perfectly symmetrical French braids without a single strand out of place. I wore a sweatshirt that I'd had since sixth grade, jeans, and my Ugg boots, with my hair down. I liked to read, while I heard that she was in a hip-hop dance troupe. We were opposites. Yet here we were, sitting in identical chairs on opposite ends of the school library.

I was becoming more and more sure that she had also gotten a note. Her unsure expression, and obvious attempts to hide it, revealed that she had not written the note, that she was just as confused as I was. I wondered if she was hoping for an adventure, too.

At 3:10, I walked over to her. "Hi, Fern," I said, "I'm Rosemary. We have Latin and orchestra together?"

She nodded, and I could tell she recognized me but wasn't quite sure what to think of me. I decided to take a gamble. "This might sound odd, but did you get a weird note the other day saying to be here?"

She looked me in the eye for a moment, as though deciding if she could trust me, and then nodded.

"I did, too. Do you think anyone's coming?"

She shrugged. "Can I see your note?" she asked.

I pulled it out of my pocket, and handed it to her. She unfolded it, and spent a while looking at it. Her brow wrinkled. "Mine's different," she said.

"It is?" I asked. "Can I see it?"

She handed me a similarly folded-up note. It was the same type of paper, with the same message, in what appeared to be the same handwriting. But the poem was different. Hers was shorter, in three brief stanzas.

> The Brain—is wider than the Sky—
> For—put them side by side—
> The one the other will contain
> With ease—and You—beside—
>
> The Brain is deeper than the sea—
> For—hold them—Blue to Blue—
> The one the other will absorb—
> As Sponges—Buckets—do—

The Brain is just the weight of God—
For—Heft them—Pound for Pound—
And they will differ—if they do—
As Syllable from Sound—

So the mystery deepened, I thought. Perhaps I would get my adventure after all.

I read the poem again. I thought it sounded familiar, and eventually I realized that it was Emily Dickinson. My mom's favorite. "I know this poem!" I exploded, with what was probably far too much enthusiasm. "It's an Emily Dickinson. I don't remember what it's called, though."

Fern nodded. "I learned about her in English last year. Aren't all her poem titles just the first lines?"

"That's right! She never titled any of her poems." This was one of the most interesting things about her. I remember asking my mother why on earth anyone wouldn't title their own poems. Mommy responded that maybe she named them, but the titles were just for her. Maybe, she said, Emily just didn't want to share them. I smiled as I remembered all the times my mother referenced the poet by her first name, almost as though they were old friends.

I glanced once more at the clock on the wall. It was almost 3:20.

Fern surprised me by speaking up. "Do you want to. . .investigate?" she asked. "Or we could just leave. I mean, it could just be someone's idea of a stupid joke."

I nodded. "I'm kind of curious. I might investigate."

She nodded. "It's a mystery," she said mischievously.

"Well this is a library, so I guess we're in the right place. I wonder if they have any poetry books." I felt dumb as the words left my mouth. It was a library. Of course they'd have poetry books.

Fern stood up and brushed off her immaculately spotless sweater. "Okay, so poems are the 800s," she mumbled, trying to get her bearings in the library. She saw my perplexed look and went on, "My sister works at a library. Her Dewey Decimal System ramblings get stuck in my brain sometimes. It's the kind of information you want to forget but somehow can't, you know?" She rolled her black-lined eyes, and I nodded, although I wasn't quite sure what she meant.

We found the poetry section pretty easily. I found a volume of Emily Dickinson, and paged through to the index of titles. I found the poem from Fern's note fairly easily. There wasn't any information about it though, which was somewhat disappointing, as I was half-expecting a note or some other indication that we had a mystery on our hands. I handed the book to Fern, and went in search of my poem, which we had even less information about. I found a general book of poetry, and a convenient index-by-first-line at the back. I looked for "sometimes when I watch trees sway," but came up with nothing. "There's nothing here. You don't recognize it, right?"

She shook her head. "You must read a lot of poetry, though, if you recognized that Dickinson one. It's not one I read in school."

I shrugged. "My mom was a poet. She read it to us a lot. Dickinson was her favorite."

"Oh, that must be cool."

I was caught off guard by her use of present tense, and I paused for a moment before nodding.

I turned back to the poetry books I had spread about on the table in front of me. I checked four more for the poem that had been on my note, to no avail. I wished I could ask my mom. I checked the clock again, realizing with a jolt that it was almost four o'clock. I had to be home soon. Audrey would be worried.

I said a hasty good-bye to Fern, and began to walk home. I pulled out my cell phone as I took the steps down to the street two at a time. I called the house phone, which had an attachment that used speech-to-text and blinking lights to indicate that there was a message, in case Audrey was home alone. There was no answer, so I left a message, and hurried home a bit quicker than usual.

My dad had invented the system when Audrey and I got cell phones for our birthday, in anticipation of the transition to school. He had a side interest in engineering, and when he wasn't at the university teaching world history, he could often be found in his office, fiddling with various materials and creating something new. I was very proud of him, especially after his invention of the phone system which simplified phone calls for everyone.

I got home at 4:10, an entire hour later than usual. Audrey seemed nonplussed at my late arrival. She was in her room, as usual, doing homework.

I'm home, I signed to her, but got no reply. *You okay?* I asked. She nodded, and went back to her book. I walked over to her. She had open books spread out on the floor in front of her, like she often did, and it struck me how it appeared as though the books were all looking to her, like an orchestra looks at its maestro. Today, however, she did not even give a passing glance to the other books on the floor. All of her attention was focused on the one she held. It was a library book, something about trees, judging by the cover. I didn't ask about it. Sometimes it was easier not to pretend I knew what she was talking about when she went into one of her scientific moods.

I went outside for a while, sitting on the back porch with my well-worn copy of The Lord of the Rings. The trees were all vivid, vibrant colors, glowing in the gold of the setting sun, and I smiled, soaking in the colors of a world that stayed the same while everything in it changed and fell to pieces and then healed itself again. I loved autumn, but this year I had somehow missed it, with school taking up so much of my time. I looked up to the tops of the trees, their fiery colors in contrast with the steady blue sky. The birds were all singing their lovely, chaotic harmonies, and I listened. It was almost melodic, the way their voices blended together: different, but at the same time, very alike.

An orchestra.

09. bEnjamin

THE DAY I LEARNED about the trees, I went for a walk with Rosemary. I have always loved walks. It is an unspoken rule of walks that no speaking is necessary. You can walk in perfect silence and it is not unusual or uncomfortable. Rosemary and I used to go for a lot of walks, but ever since Mom died, our walks had become few and far between.

She had asked me how school was when I got home, and I had asked her the same. We had both given the kinds of answers that one gives when they don't want to be asked any more questions. We set off for a walk around the neighborhood before Dad got back from the university. We walked side by side, not talking.

Parallel lines, but further apart than before.

I went on the walk to clear my mind, but it turned out to have the opposite effect. My mind swirled with trees and cats, atoms and universes and hallways full of people I couldn't talk to.

Later on, Dad came home from work about a half hour late. He sometimes stayed a little later than usual to help a student with homework, but he usually called Rosemary first. I knew Rosie was worried when he was late; I think Mom's accident had made her a little paranoid. I tried to comfort her by listing all the possible things that could've held Dad up, but I don't think it helped. Rosemary was sometimes so hard to reach sometimes.

We were both surprised when Dad came through the door, holding a squirming little bundle. Rosemary's mouth opened in shock and she ran over to where Dad stood, smiling, in the doorway. Rosemary gently took the kitten from him, bringing it over to the couch where I was sitting, and we both laughed as it stumbled on the unstable couch cushions. It was learning to walk.

Where did it come from? I frantically signed in Dad's general direction, not taking my eyes off the kitten.

He laughed. *It's kind of a long story,* he signed

slowly, watching us play with the little cat. *I thought I'd ask you girls before I brought him home, but. . .* He trailed off into laughter. *I'd been thinking about it for some time. Your mother loved cats, you know. I thought I'd bring you to the shelter and we'd pick one out together, but this one was in such bad shape and they said he wouldn't last much longer if he didn't find a family. His mother abandoned him when he was born, they told me. So what do you think?*

Rosemary's eyes were wide, her smile reaching ear to ear. *So we're keeping him?*

He nodded. *If it's alright with you two. Audrey?*

I rubbed the kitten's head. Its entire body, covered with thin gray fuzz, was barely bigger than my hand. I nodded vigorously. *Yes! Does he have a name?*

Dad shook his head. *Not yet.*

So we get to name him?

Dad nodded. *We get to name him.*

Rosie nodded slowly, obviously deep in thought. All of a sudden she laughed. *He looks just like a little dust bunny! We could call him Dusty!*

Dad shrugged. *Sure. Do you have any ideas, Audrey?*

I thought. I'd never really named anything

before. I almost signed *Schrodinger*, but this was a pet, not a science experiment. I looked closer. The kitten's eyes were a gray-green color, like the ocean during a storm. *Ocean*, I signed.

Dad tilted his head to the side. *But the ocean is blue.*

Not always.

They stared at me, not comprehending.

When I saw that they still didn't get it, I signed, somewhat impatiently, *Look at his eyes.*

Rosie took the poor kitten from my lap, holding it up so that they were eye to eye. *His eyes do look stormy*, she signed once she had put him back in my lap.

Dad shook his head. *How I came to end up with such poetic females, I'll never know. You're so much like your mother.*

After a moment, Rosemary spoke up. *Well, what do you think, Dad?*

Dad tilted his head to the side. *I don't really know.* He paused for a second, deep in thought. *Benjamin?*

The expectant look on his face was so funny that my sister and I both laughed. How he took one look at this little bundle of fur and energy and thought "Benjamin" I'll never know, but the name stuck, and we all knew we had found a name.

I like Benjamin.

Rosie was smiling. *So do I. We don't always have to torture you with our poetic tendencies, do we, Audrey? Benjamin is perfect.*

Dad started laughing even harder. Benjamin the kitten got up, went over to Dad, and proceeded to pee all over Dad's new flannel shirt and the couch cushions. Rosemary and I erupted into laughter while the kitten obliviously continued to explore the sofa.

And so began our first evening with Benjamin the kitten.

10. clues

THE KEY TO LIFE with a deaf person in the family, at least with Audrey, is knowing how to look for clues. Since she never learned verbal communication, most of her messages are conveyed through these signals that she sends, consciously or otherwise. When we were really little, she would have these tantrums whenever she was upset or sad or angry. She would flail her little arms around and scream. Mommy used to get so frustrated when she couldn't figure out what it was that Audrey wanted. She was not angry with Audrey for having a tantrum, although her patience wore thin at times. She was frustrated with her inability to understand.

As we got older, Audrey's signals became

more subtle, but Dad and I can usually figure them out.

I think that everyone sends out these same signals, even though we may not realize it. Somehow, Audrey picked up on my signals that I liked music, signals that I hadn't even realized that I was sending. When you have to rely on these signals, like I do with Audrey, you get pretty good at reading people, at solving clues in general. Or at least, that's what I like to think.

So when I got the note with the poem on it, and then was unable to locate the poem, I became determined to figure this one out. Maybe this was my one chance to solve a real mystery.

Two days after my meeting with Fern in the library, she came up to my table at lunch, a table on the literal and figurative outskirts of the cafeteria. I had ended up there on the first day, flocking towards the people I had already had classes with. I didn't know anyone very well, so I usually kept to myself during those forty minutes, sometimes bringing with me some homework to do or a book to read. Lunch had been fairly uneventful so far, so I was surprised to see Fern Reynolds sidling up to my table. Frankly, I had assumed that she had lost interest in the poems, since I had heard nothing about our meeting or about the notes for the last 48 hours. She walked up to me towards the end of lunch and tapped me on the shoulder. She glanced at my tablemates, an unlikely group of oddly talkative introverts, all of whom were chatting a mile a minute. Obviously concluding that our chance of being overheard was quite small, she sat down in the chair next to me. "Hey, Rosemary," she said.

"Hi, Fern."

"I've been thinking about that poem lately. There's this library by my house that has this huge poetry section. I've gotta go there after school anyway, so my sister can drive me home, but I thought maybe we could check it out? Maybe see if we can find any more information about the poems? You free?"

I nodded, pleasantly surprised that she seemed as interested in this as I was. "Sounds good."

"K, cool. Meet you in the courtyard at 3?"

I gave her a thumbs up, and watched her as she strutted away. Fern was the kind of girl to go to the mall with boys after school, not to search through an entire library for a single poem. I looked over to her lunch table, in the center of the cafeteria, where a rotating cast of popular kids perched on the edge of their chairs in anticipation of the latest gossip. Fern swished her hair as she sat down, the girls on either side of her absorbing her back into the fold, without pausing their conversation. I wondered if those girls knew about Fern's other side, the part that went to libraries and read poetry.

I drew my attention back to the book I was reading, wondering why this seemed to mean so much to me. It could very well be a joke, I told myself yet again. But that didn't seem to matter in the least.

In Latin, Mrs. Perez yet again began the class by speaking solely in Latin. I had chosen Latin because my mother had taken it, and I wasn't particularly interested in language except to get credit for the class. I figured that my experience with sign language might lend itself to the study of a new language, but whether it was due to Mrs. Perez's unconventional teaching methods or my own incompetence, I could not seem to understand anything relating to the language of Latin. Mrs. Perez summoned me to her desk when the bell rang, as the students were streaming out the door into the hall. "Hello, Rosemary. How are you today?"

"Good." I said flatly. I hated small talk.

"I noticed that you might be having some trouble with this class. Is that right?"

I shrugged, nodded. "Yes."

She nodded, almost sympathetically. "Do you think you might benefit from some tutoring? I could stay a couple minutes after school every day to go over it with you, if you'd like."

I sighed, and then pulled myself together, smiling politely. "Can I think about it? My schedule is pretty busy right now." It wasn't, but I didn't want to spend any more time learning Latin vocabulary than I had to. For some reason, I was violently opposed to the idea of tutoring. It was only my first semester of high school, and if it went well, it seemed as though the remaining three years would also go smoothly. Tutoring felt like giving in.

"Absolutely," she said with a smile. "Only if you think it would help you. Have a good day, Rosemary."

"You too." I turned and went out into the hallway. Once out of Mrs. Perez's view, I began to jog, not wanting to be late for the meeting in the courtyard. I hastily packed up my books and shrugged my bookbag onto one shoulder, making my way to the courtyard at the center of the Ushaped school building. Fern was already there, chatting with some friends, and I froze. Had she invited the whole crowd?

Upon noticing me, she waved to her friends and walked over to me. So it was just the two of us. "Hi, Rosemary!" she exclaimed. "You ready?"

"Hey, Fern. I'm all set."

"Awesome. Let's go."

We started walking. I looked down at my shoes as we strolled down the sidewalk. They were pretty ordinary jogging shoes, clean but not pristine, well-worn but not shabby. I glanced over at Fern's boots, tall and tightly laced, making little *click click* noises against the pavement. The shoes of an urban detective.

My head shot up as Fern addressed me. "So. I've been thinking about the poems. Do you think they have anything in common or they're just random excerpts?"

I told her about the searching I'd done at home, about my lack of any more information than we'd had before. "They're probably related in some way, if they really are clues to something. But I have no idea what the connection is."

"Me either. That's what is so weird about this. They're not even similar. I almost think it's a joke, but why would they have us go to a library of all places to make fools of ourselves? If I was playing a prank on someone, I'd probably tell them to go somewhere a bit more ridiculous."

This was true. We'd arrived at the library, an old stone, Victorian-style building I'd been in a few times with Mom years ago. There were white rocking chairs on the porch, and a rickety-looking porch swing. It didn't look much like a library from the outside, and that was what I liked the most about it. It wasn't what it seemed.

We walked in the tall double doors and breathed in the smell of used library books, which I've always loved. Fern introduced me to her sister Jenna, a tall, blue-haired girl in her twenties with a multicolored scarf, who was sitting at a desk in the back. She and her blue hair seemed slightly out of place in this library full of antiquity, but Fern had surprised me, so I wouldn't assume.

We set off for the poetry section, a cavern of shelves towards the back with comfy chairs nestled between the shelves. I stopped in the middle and slowly spun around. "Where do we even start?" I asked Fern. The shelves were so tall that I wasn't sure I could reach the top, and the section was much bigger than the school library's sad little collection of poems.

Fern shrugged. "Let's see if they have any books of poetry about trees."

We scoured the shelves for anything with "tree" in the title. We found a few books, none of which had any poems beginning with the line that my poem had begun with. After that, we began just searching through random books we pulled off the shelves. It was awfully boring, but we were strangely determined. After about fifteen searches with no success, I fell into one of the big easy chairs in the middle of the room. "We'll never find it," I muttered.

Fern sighed. She was sitting in a chair by a table, rifling through a book of T.S. Eliot poems. She stood up, walked over to a shelf, and closed her eyes. She ran her hand over the shelf and stopped on a thick black book. She pulled it out.

"How did you do that?" I asked.

She laughed. "Sometimes my sister does that when she needs a new book to read. She says that the reading gods guide her hand to the perfect book or something like that. It's stupid, but. . .you know." She shrugged mischievously. "Nothing else has worked."

I chuckled and stood up. She was right.

Nothing that we had tried so far had worked. By now my brain was coming up with the most ridiculous ideas of what the notes could point to. It had been a long day, and I was tired. So I could use some silliness.

I shut my eyes and walked towards the shelf of books, holding my hands out in front of me as a guide. I ran into the shelf more quickly than I had expected, and laughed. I ran my hand over the row of books. Some of the spines were glossy with plastic coverings, others were leather-bound, others were paper. I rested my hand on a thin book of Renaissance poetry, which I saw when I opened my eyes. I highly doubted that the poem we were after was from the Renaissance, but I looked through it, just to be sure.

By four o'clock, which was when I had told Dad and Audrey I would be leaving, Fern and I were laughing as we rifled through books. It was oddly satisfying, like we were medieval monks looking for prophecies in the sacred texts, or detectives in the decrepit streets of 19th century London. It was tedious, yet intoxicating.

I got home at 4:20. Dad wasn't home yet, and it took me a while to find Audrey. She wasn't in her room, the kitchen, or the basement. After some searching, I heard the faint humming of a violin. Perplexed, I followed the sound to my own bedroom, where I found Audrey holding my violin, drawing the bow over the strings with her eyes closed. I stood in the doorway for a while, waiting for her to open her eyes and notice me. I wondered, like many times before, what she was feeling. Unable to hear anything, with her eyes closed, what was the world like? How do you navigate with only your sense of touch?

I thought of Fern's idea of picking out books with your eyes closed. Things certainly seemed simpler that way, although that was just a minuscule window into what Audrey lived with every day.

Audrey and I had always had free rein in each others' rooms, but she'd never shown much interest in my violin before. I was intrigued, and I smiled, wondering what she was feeling.

After a few more notes that sounded rather detached and discordant, she opened her eyes wide, evidently surprised to see me.

She gently set the instrument back in its case, which lay at her feet. *Hi,* she signed, with a somewhat sheepish look on her face.

I waved. *What were you doing?* I signed. I

didn't mean it in a harsh or scolding way; I was just curious.

I just. . .wanted to feel the music again.

I nodded. I had a violin lesson the next day, a Saturday, which sparked an idea. I suddenly felt ready to share Miss Strayer with Audrey. Was it out of pity? Sympathy? Or something different? I wasn't sure. Sometimes when my mom got really excited about something she read or wrote, she would tell me and Audrey about it, even if we were too young to understand what she was talking about. Her enthusiasm was contagious, nonetheless. I thought maybe it was something like that.

Do you want to come to my lesson tomorrow? Miss Strayer has all sorts of instruments. It could be like an experiment, to see how you feel the different sounds.

She looked unsure about it until the word "experiment," and then her eyes widened infinitesimally. My sister found nothing more fascinating than scientific experiments.

She nodded. *Could I?*

I shrugged. *Sure.*

I told her about the trip to the library with Fern, leaving out the part about the notes and the whole element of mystery because I didn't really feel like explaining it all. When Audrey asked why we were there, I said it was for a school project. I think it was the first time I ever lied to her, even about something as trivial as this. I didn't like it.

But when I got to the part about searching for the books, we both laughed. It felt good to laugh with her again.

11. interpretAtions

A FEW WEEKS AFTER we got Benjamin, about a third of the way through the first semester, schoolwork started to get somewhat more intense. We had more homework, more classwork, and more class lectures. All that, combined with the increasingly cold winds, meant less time for socializing, which was quite all right with me. After the first few weeks of the school year, the excitement had worn off, and schoolwork began to feel more like work, even in the subjects I enjoyed. These days kind of blurred into a single memory of sitting, writing, reading, and occasionally dozing off. However, a few of these days stand out in my memory.

One rainy day in mid-October, the whole freshman class was called into the auditorium for an assembly. I was surprised that an assembly would take up an entire class period, since the teachers were so enthusiastic about using every single moment of school for learning, but when I arrived in the auditorium, I found that many of my teachers were already there.

I found a seat at the end of a row, away from any large groups of people, and waited for the assembly to begin. After a few moments, Mrs. Alvarez, our principal, came up to the podium with a big smile. Mrs. Alvarez was a plump, smiley woman with a somewhat conflicting air of nerves and expensive perfume. She apparently did not know sign language, and so there was an interpreter standing a little bit to the side of the podium, where Mrs. Alvarez stood, looking vaguely uncomfortable in front of so many people. The interpreter was a tall, elderly man who I had never seen before.

Hello, ninth graders, the interpreter signed dryly, translating Mrs. Alvarez's spoken words. *You are probably wondering why we brought you all here.* Students nodded all throughout the cavernous room.

IF WE FALL IN THE FOREST

You are here because you are about to become a part of a longstanding Ashton Heights High School tradition. Even though I couldn't hear the murmurs that rippled through the room, I could see them.

Every year, the interpreter went on with big exaggerated hand motions, *the freshmen of this school have participated in a project that we like to think is pretty unique to AHHS. It is an interdisciplinary project on a topic of your choice that will be presented to the school in the spring. This semester-long project combines the vital life skills of research, public speaking, and organization, just to name a few. These skills will be applied to a topic that each of you is deeply interested in, and you will spend time learning about this topic in depth.*

I would now like to introduce our ninth grade English teacher, whom you already know, Mr. Eaton.

A short bearded man, my English teacher, strolled up to the podium and bowed dramatically. He was a very dramatic man.

Good morning, ladies and gentlemen, he began. *I am here to explain the initial segment of your project, the English portion. You must in some way incorporate a work of literature into your project, and provide a detailed analysis of the piece itself and its relation to your chosen topic. You may address the theme, setting,* *character or an element of the plot. For example, if I were presenting on the topic of, say, agriculture, then I might discuss the setting of the farm in Orwell's <u>Animal Farm</u>, the symbolism of farming in Steinbeck's <u>Of Mice and Men</u>, or the importance of flashbacks to the narrator's childhood home in Wharton's <u>My Antonia</u>. Your chosen work of literature must be approved by the English department if it does not appear on the school-provided reading list you received at the beginning of the year.*

Mr. Eaton continued explaining the boring logistics of the literature portion of the project, and I rolled the idea around in my mind. I had heard of the books he mentioned, but of course I had never read them. I remembered crumpling the school-approved reading list under a bunch of math textbooks in my backpack, and assumed it was still there.

After a while, Mr. Eaton handed the microphone over to the science director, a thin woman with round glasses and hair that stuck up. She explained the research element of the project. The math director and the arts director followed suit, explaining the mathematical and artistic elements of our project.

After being provided with the information to start preliminary research on a topic of our choice, we had the opportunity to ask Mrs. Alvarez any questions we had. Hands shot up all around the auditorium.

When is this due?

Can it be about anything?

What if we're not artistic?

Are we presenting to the WHOLE school?

The questions went on and on. Mrs. Alvarez pursed her lips and addressed the mob of ninth graders. *It is due sometime in January. Yes, it can be about anything that is school-appropriate and can be tied to all the required subjects. If you aren't artistic, then you can use music, theater, dance, or some other type of fine or performing art. And, the whole ninth grade will see your presentations over a period of several weeks, and those voted the best will be presented to the entire school.*

My hands got clammy at the very thought of presenting to the 500 students of Ashton Heights High School, although I was sure my project would not be voted one of the best. While I could easily complete the math and science portions of the project, I was a bit uneasy about the English and art requirements.

I got up from my chair in the auditorium, the wood creaking in the old theater chair as I stood. I pictured my universe splitting as I considered all the options for my project. I could, of course, research the multiverse, but I already knew more than I wanted to know about that, and besides, I wasn't sure how to tie English and art to it.

Later that day, once I got off the bus and let myself in the house, I passed Rosemary's open bedroom door, and saw her violin case lying on an easy chair. I dropped my bags in my room, and went into Rosemary's. I needed to think. I'm not sure what motivated me to pick up her instrument and try to play it myself, but it seemed the most logical thing to do at the moment. I picked it up, tucking the wooden body under my chin like I'd seen Rosie do when she practiced, and began to draw the bow across the thin strings. I felt the instrument vibrating, and shivered as the vibrations found their way inside my head.

I closed my eyes and let my mind wander as I played. I couldn't experience music the same way other people could, but I could imagine what it was like for them. It seemed incomprehensible that the same tree that made this violin could very well have made a chair, or a telephone pole, or something else so much more mundane than this wonderful creation I held under my chin. I wondered what type of tree it was, and where it grew, and if it had a tree family, and if it communicated with other trees, and if it knew it would someday become a violin. My mind spiraled, and by the time I opened my eyes and found a bewildered Rosemary staring at me, I realized that I had found my research topic.

The next morning, I went with Rosemary to Miss Strayer's house for Rosie's violin lesson. The house was wonderfully cluttered with color, just like my sister had described it. In the music room, we found all sorts of instruments: strings, woodwinds, keyboards, guitars, and more that I didn't recognize. I made a mental note to ask Rosemary about them later.

Since Miss Strayer didn't know sign language, Rosemary had to translate for me, which was tedious, but necessary.

Miss Strayer seemed genuinely interested in my reaction to Rosie's violin, and suggested that we see if I can feel the vibrations from other instruments. She cleared the flat top of the baby grand piano, placing the miscellaneous objects that had cluttered it on the floor underneath, and lifted up the top. She propped up the shiny black surface with a thin wooden bar so that it was held up diagonally. She sat down at her piano, and placed my hand very lightly on the strings under the tabletop, so I could feel them without interrupting their vibrations, she explained. I had never known before that a piano had strings.

It was the same as the violin; I could feel it vibrating, even when I took my hand off the strings and just stood next to Miss Strayer as she played.

I smiled. *It feels like the wind. Or the trees blowing in a breeze.*

For the remainder of the lesson, I sat on a chair in the corner of the room as Miss Strayer and Rosemary played duets, with Miss Strayer playing one instrument, and then another, and then another, all accompanying the steady vibrations of Rosie's violin. With each instrument, the feeling was slightly different; when she played lower notes, I could feel them ringing in my chest, while higher notes made a buzzing sensation in my head.

I looked around the room as they played, savoring the strange sensations. There were instruments littering the floor and every available surface; many hung on the wall as well. In the midst of the clutter and the music, there were a few photos hanging on the wall, along with a round analog clock. I looked closer at the pictures. With everything else that was going on in the room, I wasn't even sure if I would have noticed them if I hadn't been looking around for them. They were in cheap frames, and the pictures themselves looked old and creased beneath smudged glass covers. One depicted a young mom holding a baby with thick, kinky hair in two little puffs. The photo was pretty grainy, and I assumed it was Miss Strayer as a baby, with her mother. Another showed a young man in a military uniform. This picture looked more recent than the other, and I wondered who it was.

When Rosemary's lesson was over, Miss Strayer stood up. She began talking to me, and Rosie signed to me to translate. *One more thing that I want to try,* she said. Her multicolored scarves fluttered as she walked over to her violin, and tuned it with an expert's precision. She then proceeded to tune her cello, upright bass, electric bass, harp, and a couple other stringed instruments I couldn't identify. Smiling, she walked up to me when she was done. *Are you ready?*

I was confused. *For what?*

She just smiled. She instructed Rosemary to do something, and my sister picked up her violin and struck a note. All of a sudden it felt as though the very air around me was vibrating. I could feel the sound waves moving around as though she was playing a thousand notes at once. She took her bow off the instrument, and I closed my eyes, savoring the feeling as it gradually diminished. I looked at Miss Strayer, perplexed.

What was that? I asked.

You could feel it, then? She asked with a smile.

I nodded vigorously.

If you have two perfectly tuned violins and you play one, the other will vibrate as well. I didn't know if it would work on such a big scale. What did it feel like?

I did my best to explain it, while they both watched me with fascination.

After I was finished. Miss Strayer looked at me with what seemed almost like admiration. *You have a gift, Audrey.*

The next day in English class, Mr. Eaton announced that we were beginning our unit on poetry. I inwardly groaned. Poetry was my mother's specialty, and my sister's, but it had never been mine. I had never understood the point of it. If you had something to say, why not say it in the most direct way possible? Symbolism and themes flew right over my head, not to mention the little nuances of spoken language that got lost in translation.

As instructed, I pulled my textbook out of

my bookbag. The page we were working on was devoted to Robert Frost, a poet my mother had adored, and therefore, one that I was already somewhat acquainted with. His poems, at least the ones my mother had enjoyed the most, were fairly straightforward. They told simple enough stories that I was convinced that Mom was making up all the symbolic allegories that she would always seem to pull out of thin air.

Mr. Eaton read a poem out loud, signing as he spoke. It was called "The Sound of Trees." The title intrigued me. Did trees make sounds? I thought of the violin, all the wooden instruments that had come from trees. I watched his hands move with interest. The poem portrayed trees as so alive, and while it didn't mention their communication networks, it was all that I could think about as I listened to it.

That night, I went home, dug out one of my mother's old poetry books, and found the poem. I read it over and over. What did he mean by "the sound of trees?" Was it a language, like English or American Sign? Or just a noise?

The days got shorter with the arrival of November. I began to work on my project for hours at a time. I knew that I was probably going above and beyond the requirements, but for some reason, I felt a need to dig into the language of trees as deeply as I could. Perhaps it was to feel closer to my mother. Or maybe it was because the world spoke a language that I didn't, and I felt a connection with the speaking trees. I didn't know exactly why, but I became more and more desperate in my search as the days went by.

12. drifting (qUestioning)

WHEN AUDREY AND I were really little, our parents took us to the beach for the first time. We had never seen the ocean before, and its vast glittery openness was more beautiful than I had ever imagined. While I loved to sit and look at it, I was hesitant to go in the water, but Audrey was not. In fact, Mommy had to restrain her from going in as far as she wanted to go, which was far deeper than I would have dared. I stayed mostly on land, playing with Dad, but the one time I did go in the water, I got really scared. Mommy was focused mainly on Audrey, since she had to stay close. I sort of just lifted my feet off the sandy floor and floated. I had assumed that it would be like at the pool, where you just stay in place as you float, but when I looked up, I could barely even see Mommy and Audrey. I think I screamed, but the memory is pretty vague. I know that Mommy felt bad for leaving me on my own, and I remember the next time we went to the beach, she made Dad go in the water with me, so there would be one grown-up for each of us.

I still remember that feeling so clearly, though, like a nightmare you don't ever forget. The feeling that you've drifted so far away from where you began, but don't even realize it. When Audrey and I went to school, the same thing happened. We were drifting away from each other, but I don't think either of us noticed.

October passed, with November close behind. Mr. Alden called for more intense orchestra rehearsals for the concert in early December. Every other day, we met in the orchestra hall to practice, and I spent less and less time at home. It was as though the ocean waves were swelling and receding more rapidly, the water moving faster and longer and wider.

The orchestra hall was quickly becoming my favorite part of the school. It was high-ceilinged, and almost medieval, like we were in a monastery rather than a school. I'm not sure Sherlock Holmes ever solved a mystery in a private high school, but in a medieval monastery, anything seemed possible.

Over the next few weeks, Fern and I crossed paths a couple times and asked whether the other had made any progress in our search, but aside from that, she acted as though she barely knew me. She was never rude, but never went out of her way to include me, either. Maybe we were drifting, too.

And as for Audrey, she was becoming more reclusive than ever. My sister had always been quiet, but as my school life brought me further out of my shell, Audrey seemed to be receding further and further into her mind.

One day in late October, I went into Audrey's room after finishing my homework. Once she got home from school, she spent much of the evening alone. Most days, I barely saw her unless I went in to visit. She was usually reading, or studying, or occasionally drawing, but on this particular day, I slipped in the door, and saw her sitting on the floor in front of a chessboard, all set up for a game.

Hey Audrey, I signed. *What are you doing?*

She shrugged.

Do you want to play?

She shook her head.

Just. . . . studying the board?

She nodded. I wished I could understand what went on in her mind. We used to be able to know what the other was thinking without even signing. It was like that day at the beach. The waves had carried me one way, and Audrey another.

The next day, I was scheduled to have my first tutoring session with Mrs. Perez. I had signed up rather reluctantly after a lecture from my dad involving the importance of trying one's best. I had conceded, in the end, so that he would stop talking.

So, in the half hour between the end of the school day and the start of orchestra rehearsal, I peeped my head into Mrs. Perez's room. Even though she had invited me, I still felt a little intimidated by her and wanted to avoid barging in on some unrelated business.

Unfortunately, she seemed to be caught up in just that. As I cracked the door open, the sound of a phone conversation drifted tinnily into the hallway. I closed the door as gently as I could, but not before I overheard some legal-sounding terms coming from Mrs. Perez's end. Her voice was raised, and she seemed agitated.

"There's really nothing you can do?

Nothing?!" Mrs. Perez's angry outburst took me by surprise, and I moved further from the door, so she wouldn't think I had been eavesdropping. After all, I hadn't been.

My mind wandered as I waited outside the door, far enough away so that I couldn't overhear anything more, but close enough so that she would see me if she came looking for me. I sat on the hard tile floor, and felt the cool cinder block against the back of my head. I wondered who she was on the phone with, and why. She certainly seemed distressed. What if she was in trouble?

Just as I was beginning to consider creeping closer to the door, Mrs. Perez opened it and ventured into the hallway. "Hello, Rosemary," she said cheerfully. "So sorry for the delay. I had to make a phone call."

She ushered me in the room, and dragged a chair over from a student's desk to her own. She sat in her swivel chair, and patted the student's chair. I went over and sat down. "So," she said, "I am well aware that Latin is not a subject that many students enjoy." At my instinctual feigned look of surprise, she chuckled. "I am not offended, or even surprised. I've been teaching long enough. My daughter hated it, as a matter of fact." She chuckled again, but with less enthusiasm this time.

"So," she said gently, "Let's get down to business."

She placed a Latin worksheet in front of me, and stood up to write something on the chalkboard. As she stood up, a gold-framed photo on her desk caught my eye. It showed a little, puff-haired baby being held by a young woman, who looked like a younger version of Mrs. Perez. I wondered if this was the daughter that she had referenced earlier, the one who hated Latin.

I didn't want Mrs. Perez to think I was not paying attention, even though I wasn't. I was trying my best, but focusing was not one of my strong points. Besides, Mrs. Perez did not seem to me the type of person who enjoys having near-strangers browse her personal pictures, so I quickly turned my eyes back up at her. But she had already noted my interest in the photo, and was looking at it intently herself. "My daughter," she said flatly. "She's all grown up now."

I smiled, unsure of what to say. Before I could decide on something, she cleared her throat. "Anyway. Let's begin. Do you remember the basic conjugation rules?"

As we went on with the Latin lesson, which

made only slightly more sense than when she explained it in class, my mind wandered. I tried to pay attention, but the mystery of the poem and all the orchestra music and Mrs. Perez's angry phone call and the photo of the baby were all swimming around in my brain, vying for my attention. I wondered what her daughter was doing now.

The tutoring session finally ended, just as I was beginning to think it never would. I thanked Mrs. Perez, took one last sideways glance at the photo that had warranted such a strange reaction, and scrambled up to my locker for my violin. I took the stairs two at a time, inwardly cursing my hard-soled uniform shoes as I came within an inch of slipping on the tiled steps. Every girl at St. Mike's tripped on the stairs on account of these darn shoes at least once a semester, and a quick glance at my watch told me that I would be a few minutes late for orchestra already. I prayed that Mr. Alden would be looking away as I came in the door, remembering the toxic glare he'd given Fern on that first day, the day we'd gotten the notes.

Despite my fear of being late, I stopped in my tracks just outside the orchestra hall as something occurred to me. What if Mr. Alden had sent us those notes? He was the one who had handed the folders out, after all. Why would he have done that, though? Especially since no one had shown up that day in the library.

"Miss Cooper?" came a cold, thin voice from a little ahead of me. My head jerked upwards.

Mr. Alden raised a wiry eyebrow at me. "Would you care to come in, Miss Cooper? Or were you planning on standing outside for the whole rehearsal?"

I looked at him in slight shock, sputtered, "I was just - I'm coming in," and hurried inside, as he held the door open for me with an imposing, slightly condescending look.

After an hour of intense rehearsal, we were dismissed. Days passed rather uneventfully. The date of December 10th crept closer and closer. I spent hours on my violin at home, practicing. I went for hours sometimes without seeing Audrey. She had been somewhat reluctant to tell me what had been going on at her school, but I knew she had a big project coming up that required a lot of work.

I was surprised by how invested she seemed in school. Her studies had always been an important part of her life, but most of it had been outside the curriculum. It occurred to me suddenly that I hadn't told her much about what went on at my school, either.

I had thought that it was only my sister who was drifting away from me, but perhaps I was moving, too.

13. stillness

A WEEK BEFORE Rosemary's concert, I went to the school library to work on my project. Since the bells that my school used to separate class periods obviously did not work for some of us, the maintenance staff had installed a system of flashing lights that went off when the bells rang. It always took me by surprise, when the white lights began blinking spasmodically in the corner of the ceiling.

Once dismissed by the lights, I retreated to the library for lunch, where I set up my materials on my favorite table in the corner by the back window. It was like every other table in the library, but it was partially hidden by a shelf of nonfiction books covering topics I happened to be very interested in. I restrained myself from picking one off the shelf, and forced myself to think about my project. I had finished my science experiment, planting two small trees in a big pot and one in a smaller one. I introduced a harmful chemical to one of the trees in the larger pot and the one in the smaller one. If the experiment was successful, then the sick tree in the bigger pot would stay healthier longer than the tree in its own pot, for the healthy tree would transport nutrients to the sick tree in the same container. I had also completed the mathematical and research elements, explaining the value of the number e, which played a role in the growth of trees, among other natural processes. However, I still did not understand how English could be tied to such a scientific topic. They seemed to me complete opposites.

So I retreated to one of my favorite spots, a soft place in stark contrast to the chaos of the rest of the school. The library was furnished with white chairs that were simple but comfortable, and smelled like coffee and old books. I didn't often go there to read, or even to study, but just to sit. When all you've known is home, it's hard to go alone into the angular, fluorescent lights of public school. I needed the stillness.

During the first week of school, I had begun to go to the library nearly every day, even if it was only to sit and think. I've seen Rosemary sign about how it is sometimes overwhelming to be in a room with a lot of people talking at the same time. It's funny how I can have this same experience, but without the noise. I am very familiar with the concept of silence, even though I have never known sound. And so I go to the library to be alone, which is always easier, I've found.

After a while, I crept behind a shelf so that rows of books rose like trees on either side of me. I was reading a new article I had found on tree communication. A lot of what I had found was already familiar, considering the vast number of articles, stories, and blog posts I had already read. So I was a little surprised to find an entirely new bit of information. "Trees use their fungal root networks to communicate, by sending nutrients to their allies or even sabotaging their enemies," I read.

Sabotaging their enemies? Up until now, I had been picturing trees as benevolent sentinels of the woods. What does a tree have to do to become the enemy of another?

This shouldn't bother me, I thought. It had

nothing to do with me. But if everything was connected, like Hugh Everett and Erwin Schrodinger believed, then it did. It did matter, and it had everything to do with me. I swallowed hard, bracing myself for the inevitable storm. If trees could sabotage through their roots, what sorts of evil could people commit? If the tall, beautiful giants of our planet could *sabotage*, then what were *we* capable of?

My mind swirled into a dark and turbulent whirlpool. *Sabotaging. Underground systems. Subconscious language. Poisoned roots. Evil. Good and bad. Alive and dead. Keep the cat in the box. Don't make a choice. Don't open the box. Don't leave. Don't go there. Don't stay here.*

Stay in the box. Stay in the box. Stay in the box.
Stay
in
the
box.

I'm not sure how long I sat in the library like that, in somewhat of a trance, hidden behind a shelf that couldn't in any way protect me, but some vague measure of time later, the flashing lights of the bell cut through the haze, dismissing me to my next class.

I walked through the rest of the day as though I was walking through fog. I couldn't distract my brain from the same thoughts that kept spinning around like a broken record. I couldn't control my brain; I couldn't control my life. I was not in control.

I was the cat in the box with the radioactive chemicals, and I didn't know who was running the experiment.

14. chess and (s)worDplay

THE NIGHT AFTER my first tutoring session with Mrs. Perez, I dreamt that I was in a game of chess. I hadn't played in years; it was my mother's favorite game, even though she never once beat Audrey, and I don't even think she ever went easy on her. Audrey still plays with Dad sometimes, but he isn't as good at it as Mommy was, and I was never good enough to stand a chance against either of them.

In my dream, I was on a chessboard, but instead of the usual array of pieces, there were only pawns. I was a pawn, and so were Audrey, Dad, Fern, Miss Strayer, Mrs. Perez and other classmates, teachers, and friends.

A chessboard is set up rather simply, with

119

alternating colors on adjacent squares in each row. Black and white, black and white, black and white. But the other strange thing was that every piece kept changing color. In an ordinary game of chess, there is a white team and a black team, or at least two distinct colors. In the dream, each piece was an ambiguous shade of gray- no two pieces the same color at any given time.

Suddenly the pieces began to shift, moving in ways that pawns were not supposed to move. And suddenly we were no longer on a chessboard, but performers on a stage. And then, trees in a forest. The setting kept changing, but the game was always the same.

Each chess piece was holding something like a weapon. One pawn held a sword, another a flower, another a pen. Each one wielded their object as though marching into battle. As the game progressed, each piece traded with another. The flower-pawn would switch with the sword-pawn, and all the while, the colors were shifting, swirling, changing. Eventually all the pieces had been mixed up so much that I couldn't tell who was who. It was terribly disorienting.

I had never liked chess all that much, but in the dream, it was frightening. It was all the things we were afraid to say, afraid even to think. It was all the things that happened beneath the surface of our heads, spilled out onto this strange checkered battleground.

I thought of a book I had once read, Through the Looking Glass. It is the sequel to Alice's Adventures in Wonderland, in which Alice steps through a mirror, and finds herself in a world where everything is backwards. It had never made much sense to me until now, when I was asleep, trapped in the world where the unseen was seen and the underground made visible. There were some things, I thought, better left unsaid, better left unseen.

As I thought that, from somewhere far far away, the board shifted beneath me. At first, I thought I was in water, with the waves shifting ominously beneath me; but after a moment I realized that it was a mirror, clear and dark as the ocean.

I watched as all the other pawns fell into the murky glass, but I stood suspended above them all, in the air above the mirror ocean, as everyone else fell through the looking glass. I wondered: was I stuck in the backwards-land alone, or was I the only one in the real world? And was there really any way to tell?

For some reason, the dream was almost a nightmare. I couldn't pinpoint what aspect of it scared me, but I woke up in a sweat, breathing hard.

I glanced at my alarm clock. There was only half an hour until I had to get up, and my dream had woken me up enough that I doubted I could get back to sleep. It was one of those dreams that was really hard to stop thinking about, even after you woke up. I kept thinking about the colors. In a regular chess game, each team is a specific color. When I played with Audrey, I was always the black team and she was the white. I remember one time I made her switch with me because I was convinced that it was the pieces that allowed her to win every time. Needless to say, she still won every time.

The one thing I dislike most about bad dreams is that even though you recognize how irrational your fear is, that doesn't stop it from scaring you. Even in the most absurd fantasy, there is some reality.

15. seven miles

SEVEN MILES IS the distance that the average tree can communicate to other trees. Coincidentally, it is also the distance between our house and the Ashton Heights Town Center and Auditorium. My sister's winter concert was tomorrow, and I was not going.

I was not going to complete my project, either. I was going to sit in my house and try not to think. I would not make any new decisions, and I would stay in my box. Then nothing bad would happen to me.

I brought this up during breakfast the next day. *I'm not feeling well,* I signed.

Dad and Rosemary exchanged a concerned look. *What's wrong?* Dad signed at the same moment Rosie signed, *Do you think you can come to the concert?*

Not meeting their eyes, I shrugged. *Why would I go to a concert?* My sister's eyes were wide, and I knew that I had hurt her. *I want to, Rosie. But I can't.* And this was true.

What's wrong? Dad asked again, looking me square in the eye, which he knew I didn't like.

My stomach hurts, I said, and at their slightly suspicious looks I added, *a lot.*

Audrey, are you sure you can't go? You know how hard your sister has been practicing for this.

A part of me wanted to go, to experience the vibrating air again like I had at Miss Strayer's. I wanted to see Rosemary perform. But I kept thinking about all the people there, all the people who couldn't understand me, and who I couldn't understand, and the thought kept coming back: *stay in the box.* If I went out, something could go horribly wrong. Or worse, I could do something horribly wrong. I had to stay.

I'm sorry.

Rosemary sighed and nodded. *I hope you feel better.* I could tell she was still disappointed.

After breakfast, I went straight to my room. I stayed there for most of the day, reading, drawing, thinking, and cuddling with Benjamin, who had taken a liking to me.

A few hours later, I felt the floor creaking. Rosemary was beginning to get ready. For some reason, my heart started pounding, as though trying to warn me of something. I tried my best to ignore it, but it persisted.

I pictured what Rosemary must have been doing: tuning her instrument, getting into the black dress she had bought especially for the concert, brushing her hair, sweeping it up into some fancy knot she had learned how to do at her fancy school: a knot that my frizzy brown mane would never have tolerated, but that fit her silky hair perfectly. I pictured the orchestra: dozens of girls with shiny hair done up in the latest styles, tuning their instruments with practiced precision, and handsome, prep-school boys with crooked smiles and slicked-back hair playing guitars that cost more than all the furniture in my bedroom.

Rosemary walked in, sporting her nice dress, with her hair in a simple ponytail. *Well, this is it,* she said. I nodded.

Hey, are you ok? She asked after a brief hesitation. *You've been super quiet lately.*

I considered how to respond, imagining all

the ways the world could fall apart if I said the wrong thing. In the end, I shrugged. *School's been busy,* I signed.

You'll have to tell me about it sometime. I've hardly heard anything from you!

This was true. And neither had Dad. It wasn't as though they hadn't asked; I had just chosen to keep most of my experiences to myself.

I know. Have a good concert! I signed, with as much enthusiasm as I could muster.

She gave me a quick, hard hug. *Thanks so much. You're the best.*

Her ponytail swished as she turned to go out the door, her dress twirling elegantly. She grinned as she waved goodbye. Dad came in a few minutes later, and we had the same conversation I had had with Rosemary. I promised to tell them more about school, and wished them a good trip. Once they were gone, I relaxed a little, though I wasn't quite sure why.

For a little while, I stayed curled up on my bed, reading a book, petting the cat's furry little head as he purred with pleasure. I thought about the universe splitting as I decided to stay home. I had decided to stop deciding, and every day I would decide to continue. Was there no way to stop reality from breaking?

There was a world out there, somewhere, sometime, in which I had gone to the concert. There was a world out there where I had enjoyed the concert. There was a world out there where I could hear the music like everybody else. There was a world out there where I had never read about trees, and there was a world out there where Schrodinger had never theorized about cats. There was a world out there where Schrodinger's theory had been proven. There was a world out there where everything had been proven.

Wait.

Schrodinger's cat theory had never been proven. It was just that - *a theory*. If someone could prove that the cat was either alive or dead at any given time, and not both, then we lived in only one reality. Life could be simple, and decisions wouldn't mean anything.

It was hot in my bedroom, and stuffy with all the curtains closed, but as I looked down at the cat dozing off on my lap, my mind swirling, I shivered.

I'm sorry.

16. closing

DAD AND I SAID a quick goodbye to Audrey, making sure she was okay to stay home alone, and then I shut the door behind me, jumping a little at the noise. *So this is it*, I thought.

As Dad and I drove off for my concert in silence, I couldn't stop thinking about Audrey. She rarely got sick, and even when she did, she would have never missed out on this. The unspoken agreement of twinhood says that we're there for one another. I was worried about her, although I couldn't pinpoint the exact reason. It was as though something in her was closing up. *Stop worrying*, I told myself. *If she doesn't want to come, she doesn't want to come.*

So why did I get the feeling that something was wrong?

The foreboding feeling lingered as we pulled into the parking lot. I said a quick Hail Mary, though I wasn't sure why. Whether it was for Audrey or me didn't seem to matter.

Dad dropped me off at the auditorium, and parked the car to wait until the doors opened to visitors. I grabbed my violin case, and stepped through the auditorium doors like a soldier going to battle.

I went in, and found Fern in the seat next to mine. We chatted for a while about unimportant topics, and as our conversation died down, I could tell that we both had bigger things on our minds.

After a while, Mr Alden came in, and organized the gaggle of students into our assigned seats. He handed out our folders, after having us turn them in yesterday, lest one of us forgot it today. I shuddered to think about what kind of wrath Mr. Alden would unleash on us if we were so careless.

Half an hour later, parents began streaming into the auditorium: an ocean of people whispering small talk. I was nervous, hidden behind the heavy red curtain, waiting for it to rise and let in the too-bright spotlights that would obscure my view of my dad, and the music stands that wouldn't hide my face as much as I would have liked. Fern, to my surprise, seemed nervous, too. Just as nervous as me, actually. None of her other friends were in orchestra, and it seemed like I was the only person she knew really well. Not that I knew her. I was beginning to doubt if anyone at school *really* knew her. It was funny how the most popular girl at school could be enshrouded in such mystery.

I wondered if that was part of the reason I had chosen orchestra. It allowed for anonymity.

Mr. Alden directed us to our seats, arranged in a semicircle around his music stand, where he would be conducting us.

And all of a sudden, the curtain began to rise. I took a deep breath.

I waited for Mr. Alden's command, watching his outstretched hand intently. On command, I drew my bow across the lowest string: the first note. As I went on with the piece, I thought about my sister. She would love to be here, I knew, and not just to see me play. Even I could feel the vibrations as thousands of sound waves reverberated against the walls of the theater. It was beautiful. We played *Carol of the Bells*, and then our other songs. Even though I couldn't see any of the visitors through the haze of the bright lights, I could feel their presence. It struck me how vastly different performing for an audience was than performing alone. It gave the music a different purpose, somehow. A bigger, more important one.

A little while later (I had very little sense of time while playing - it was as though the spotlight had sucked away my sense of progressing time), we stood up and took a collective bow. As we basked in the adoration of the people, the curtain began to close. Something inside me closed at that moment. I thought about Audrey, and her mind, her closing mind. The curtain hit the floor with a soft *thud*, and in that moment, I knew something was wrong. I could feel it in my bones, with a clarity I had never experienced before.

17. expeRiments

THE THING ABOUT EXPERIMENTS is that we think they can prove things, but really, they can't. Nothing about the world can ever really be proven. Not in this world, anyway. I wasn't sure about the others.

I was thinking about this as I dug out a cardboard box from the basement. I was feeling kind of mentally numb, like I had gone into some scientific trance in which emotions didn't exist. I wished I could feel like that all the time. Emotions only complicate things.

I knew that what I was doing was wrong. I knew it deep down inside, but the only thing I could focus on was that if I could show that the cat in the box could not be dead and alive at the same time, then I knew that I was not dead and alive at the same time. I would be Audrey Jean Cooper, singular, not one of an infinite number of vastly different Audrey Jean Coopers that I would never know. But they were me. The worst part of this awful world is that you can never know anything for sure. Not even yourself.

My hands were trembling as I scooped up Benjamin from his bed. I loved him. I really did. He understood me in a way that Rosemary and Dad never had. But something inside me needed to do this.

I had not previously had a plan, but everything fell into place in my head. I walked slowly into the bathroom, my thoughts uncannily clear, and dug out a mercury thermometer. I stuck the thermometer in my pocket and locked myself in my room. A moment later, something compelled me to unlock the door, though it remained tightly shut. My heart was pounding against my ribs, and I felt a weird vibrating sensation in my head, almost like music, but not quite. I distantly wondered if I was going crazy.

My mom had been a poet. My dad was a history professor. My sister - well, I'm not sure what she was, but she would not be a scientist, I knew. I was the black sheep. Maybe I wasn't even a sheep at all. I was nothing but a specimen of the scientists I idolized.

My hands were cold, and I rubbed them together, but it didn't seem to help. I petted Benjamin's head as he purred against my hand, and I marveled at how much he loved me, even now.

I opened the box. My heart pounded.

I put Benjamin in the box. My hands shook.

I placed the thermometer next to the little cat. Benjamin looked up at me with wide eyes that should have been asking for mercy, but they were clear and calm. He was so innocent he didn't know how to ask for mercy.

I closed the box. My breath came in short gasps.

And I duct-taped the box closed.

18. driving at night

I'VE ALWAYS ENJOYED car rides, especially at night, when you can curl up in the backseat and let the gentle whirring of the car lull you to sleep. When I was little, I loved to close my eyes during nighttime car rides, and try to figure out where we were. It was always a little unsettling once I finally lost track of where we were. I would open my eyes and be completely surprised to find that the neighborhood I had always lived in was strangely unfamiliar. Even so, I never felt as safe as I did during those car rides, with Dad and Mom in front and Audrey beside me. I used to pretend to be asleep so that one of my parents would carry me inside, even when I was far too old for that. I missed that feeling.

I tried to relax, laying my head against the window as Dad showered all sorts of compliments upon me. The evening had been as crazy as it was exhilarating, and my head was beginning to hurt. I still felt an odd urgency to get home, as though something was seriously wrong with Audrey.

"I can't believe you just performed in a *concert*, Rosie," Dad said, shaking his head. "You were amazing. Your mom. . ." His voice broke. "Your mom would have been so proud. Is so proud of you."

Under normal circumstances, I would have reacted differently, but tonight I simply nodded. "I know," I said distantly, trying to think of a way to bring up Audrey without sounding panicky. I hesitated. "Dad, do you ever get a feeling like you just know something is wrong? Like something is . . .out of place, almost?"

Even though it was dark, and I could barely see him, I could feel his concerned look boring into me. "I'm not sure. Is something wrong?"

I considered it. I thought something was, but I couldn't be sure. It was just a feeling, after all. "Have you noticed something weird with Audrey lately?" I eventually asked.

After a long moment he nodded. "She's been a lot quieter lately. Almost. . .reclusive."

Reclusive was a good word for it, I thought.

"Do you think she's all right?" I asked tentatively.

He sighed. "All right means something different for everyone. As you know," he added with a sideways glance at me, "she can be so hard to reach sometimes. As if she doesn't even want to be reached. But, I'm sure she'll work it out. She's stronger than she thinks. And we'll help her however we can, hm?"

I nodded, hoping that would be enough.

I thought about that for a bit. Sometimes I wanted to be out of reach, but even in those moments I was transparent, my emotions fully displayed on my face. But when Audrey wanted to be alone, she retreated into her mind, where no one could coax her out. She would go have some alone time, and then come out later looking to play chess, or go into town, or watch a movie. But nowadays, she seemed to be stuck in there all the time.

19. mEow

"This is how the world ends. Not with a bang, but with a whimper."
-T.S. Eliot

MEOW. BENJAMIN'S WHIMPER was so low and reverbative that I could feel it. All of a sudden I snapped back into reality.

I gasped, tore the tape off the box with a *rrrip.* What was I thinking?

I scooped Benjamin out of the box, and thank God, saw the thermometer lying unbroken on the bottom of the box. I held the kitten to my chest as hard as I dared, and buried my face in his fur, moaning in disgust at myself.

What had I expected? Was I really crazy enough to kill my own cat? I was crazy. Heartless and crazy. And I shouldn't be trusted with Benjamin, or with Rosemary, or with anyone.

Would I have really followed through with it? I hoped with everything I had that I was not that kind of person, but how could I be sure? Rosemary would hate me forever. Dad would hate me forever. I would die alone in a psych ward somewhere far away, and no one would remember me.

How had I even planned to prove my point? If the most accomplished physicists of the last century hadn't been able to solve it, how had I expected to? I pounded my fist into my forehead. Stupid. Stupid, crazy Audrey. What would Dad and Rosemary think of me?

My mind went around and around and around and around and around.

After a while, I felt a warm wetness in Benjamin's fur, and I realized that I was sobbing. I hugged him harder, harder and harder, until I could feel his little heart beating, pounding just as fast as mine. I could feel his purring, a futile attempt to comfort me. I was crazy. I couldn't be comforted. I cried and cried until I had cried an ocean, and when I was done, Benjamin was soaked with my tears and I was empty inside.

20. stars (crYing)

When I got out of the car to go inside that night, the first thing I noticed was the stars, which were unusually bright. There was no moon visible in the sky. A strange thought popped into my head as I looked into the sky: *what if we're all just part of one big experiment and the stars are just holes in the sky for other people to watch us?* For some reason, that really scared me, and it seemed strangely, frighteningly possible as I stared into outer space. There could be any kind of world out there. I turned my eyes away from the sky with a shiver and went inside.

I opened the door to silence. That was normal. That was good. I ventured further in, scolding myself with every step I took. *Everything is fine. What on earth were you worried about?*

I opened Audrey's bedroom door and stepped inside. Her back was turned to the door, and she was shaking, rocking back and forth with Benjamin cradled in her lap. "Audrey!" I said out loud, slowly going over to her so as not to startle her. *Are you okay?* She was sobbing. I hadn't seen her cry in years. She didn't respond. *Audrey. What's wrong?* My hands were moving frantically. Something was wrong, something was wrong, something was wrong. "Dad!" I yelled.

He came running in a moment later. I sat down on the floor and put my arms around her. Still she cried, silent tears streaming down her face into the fur of Benjamin, who lay contentedly in her lap as she clutched his little body as if her life depended on it.

I had often wondered why Benjamin had become so attached to my sister. It occurred to me for the first time that maybe she needed him more than I did. I had a feeling that she confided more in the cat than in the rest of us. I realized suddenly that maybe the cat understood my sister more than I did, and that frightened me.

Dad sat down on her other side. *Audie,* he

signed, as frantic as I was, but trying not to show it. *What happened? Are you sick?*

Audrey shook her head violently, took a deep breath, stared at the floor in front of her.

I looked around. A cardboard box lay on the floor in front of her, and a thermometer. *Were you doing an experiment for school?* I asked.

She shook her head again, harder, curling her shoulders into her body as if trying to be as small as possible. I looked down at Benjamin. She was holding him very tightly, and droplets of water shone on his dark fur, reflecting the lamplight so they looked like stars. I thought of a book that I had once read, <u>The Little Prince</u>. A few chapters in, the narrator is in a position to cry if there ever was one. His plane has crashed, he has food to last a week, and he has come upon a child in the middle of the desert. As the little prince cries over something the narrator cannot understand, the narrator muses on how difficult a task it is to comfort.

"It is such a secret place, the land of tears."

Dad looked at me over her head. He was exhausted. It was late. Audrey was upset about something we did not understand. With a deep breath, he began to rub her back, a rhythmic, circular motion that reminded me in a strange way of "Carol of the Bells," the song I'd been playing on my violin just an hour ago, though it felt like so much longer.

We huddled there for a while. Audrey hadn't had any major breakdowns since Mom died. In fact, I'm not sure I had even seen her cry since before Mom died. It was as though all of her sorrows from the past years had built up until she couldn't hold any more.

But here it was, pouring out of her with such frightening intensity.

Dad whispered to me, "Give us a moment." I nodded and stood up, though I didn't want to leave them.

I crept out of the room and not knowing quite what to do, went outside. It was darker than it had been when we got home, and warm for December, so I lay down in the middle of the lawn, letting the dew soak through my hair. I realized only then that I was still wearing my fancy black dress. I was feeling reckless, so I let my hair out of its ponytail, and lay back down. It struck me how odd it must look. I was all dolled up in my best dress, laying in the grass in the dark. It was like a movie set, and I had no idea what was happening backstage, or what the next scene would hold.

I took a deep breath. I had always loved night air. It seems to have a strange quality to it, not like color or temperature, but something else that we don't have words to describe. It was wilder, somehow.

The stars seemed to get brighter and brighter as my eyes got used to them. It's funny how everyone says you can't see many stars in the suburbs, but the truth is that those people just don't look for long enough. The stars are there, but you don't see them at first.

I ran over the events of the last few minutes in my head. I realized that when I walked in Audrey's room, my first instinct was to call her name. I wasn't sure I had ever done that before. It was strange how just a few months could change me in that way. I lived in the world of sound now.

I thought about a lot of things, all at once, stars and darkness and moonlight and music and the twisted justice of everything. And then, another thought crept in just outside the frame of my consciousness. I tried to repress it, but it fought through. Tonight was supposed to be my night. Ten years from now, I was supposed to think back fondly of my first concert, the support from Audrey and my dad in the audience, and from my mom, looking on from wherever she was.

But of course, I couldn't think that. It wasn't Audrey's fault. It wasn't anyone's fault, but here we were.

It always strikes me how things are different at night. These were things I wouldn't dare to think in the daylight, but in the cover of the stars, the thoughts felt natural.

I sighed in contentment. The cool air felt good, and my head didn't hurt as much as it had. I looked over at the house, where I saw shadows moving around in the living room. Good. So Dad had managed to get Audrey out of her room.

I stood up, surprised to feel that the dew had begun to settle on my face. With a jolt, I realized I had been crying.

It is such a secret place, the land of stars.

21. rootS: part one

AFTER A WHILE, my mind calmed down, but I could still feel the tears streaming down my face. My thoughts were strangely clear, as though the tears had washed my mind in some way.

My clutch on poor Benjamin loosened, and he scurried away in his kitten-like scamper. I watched him go.

After a while, the bright lights of the room became bearable again, and I lifted my head.

Dad looked me in the eye. I braced myself for the onslaught of questions, but they never came. He smiled. *Want some water?*

I slowly nodded, and he helped me up.

I sat down in the living room and while Dad

filled a glass from the kitchen faucet. I wondered where Rosemary had gone.

Dad came back into the living room and sat next to me on the couch.

Do you want to talk?

I shook my head. Not yet. *How was the concert?* Benjamin came back into the room, and having apparently forgiven me for my attempted stunt, climbed up on my lap. As I curled up on the couch, the strange mental clarity I had experienced before returned, but this time it was a comfort. There was a beauty in simple conversations, a healing beauty.

Dad sighed. *Pretty amazing, actually. Rosie worked hard.*

I nodded. *I know. She didn't mess up at all?*

He shook his head. For some reason I couldn't place, a weight lifted off my shoulders. Seven miles, I thought. Our roots were still intertwined.

22. Strings

I CAME BACK INSIDE to find Dad and Audrey sitting on the couch, chatting as though nothing unusual had occurred. They both laughed when I came into the room. Between the puzzled look on my face, my wet dress, and my rumpled hair that probably had leaves in it, I must've been quite a sight.

After a moment, I laughed too. I laughed and laughed and laughed. It had been a roller coaster of an evening. After a while I went to change into my pajamas, and sat down next to Audrey when I came back out. We laughed together about silly little things, like we used to, before we started school. Those days seemed like so long ago, though they were only a couple of months back.

What I hadn't realized, though, was how much things had changed within my family. Dad and Audrey and I stayed up late talking, and I was shocked by how much I hadn't known. I hadn't been aware that Dad was being honored at the next University Scholars meeting, or that he was teaching Benjamin to do tricks, or that Audrey had been spending so much time on her school project, which seemed like kind of a big deal. I told them about the poem, and Fern, and our library visits that turned up empty. Dad was surprised to hear about all my adventures, and his eyes crinkled with concern for a moment, but he relaxed as I explained how we had found a dead end. The conversation then drifted back to quieter topics. We talked about our teachers, our classmates, and Dad's coworkers, and what books we were reading, and how we would spend winter vacation, and it was wonderful.

We didn't talk about Audrey's episode, or my weird feeling in the car, or the fact that Benjamin seemed to gravitate towards Audrey for most of the night. And we didn't ask. I knew that we would explain those things in their own time. I knew that for the time being, we were okay, and that offered a strange but sufficient comfort.

I thought about Miss Strayer's room full of instruments, and the beautiful sounds that arced across the room when she tuned them perfectly. I smiled as I remembered how one instrument vibrating could cause another to vibrate across a room and make such a beautiful sound. My family and I had been out of tune for a while, but we were still making music. I could almost hear the violins as we talked.

It was a messy, disorganized symphony, but it was beautiful.

ELISE STANKUS

part 3. winter

"A murmur in the trees - to note -
not loud enough for wind -
a star - not far enough to seek -
nor near enough to find"

-Emily Dickinson

ELISE STANKUS

23. epiphany

MY MOTHER'S FAMILY is from Alaska. Her mother, my grandmother, belongs to the Tlingit tribe of the city of Hoonah. When she was a young girl, she met my grandfather, the son of Catholic missionaries living in the next town over. They were married young, and my mom grew up in a combined world of Tlingit and Catholic traditions, set in the frigid winters and vivid summers of southern Alaska. She often said she wouldn't have changed a thing.

She always loved cold weather, and said it reminded her of home. Over the years, she taught me to love it too. I learned to miss the wild wind of her homeland, even though I had only been there a handful of times. Her memories became my own, and I loved to stand outside in the snow with her, all bundled up, and listen to her stories. We used to laugh at Rosemary and Dad, clad in pajamas on the couch, cradling cups of cocoa. My sister thought I was crazy for liking the cold, and Mommy would always smile. "They can have summer," she said to me once, "but winter is our season."

As mid-December rolled around, I spent more and more time outside, as my dad and sister prepared to hunker down for the next few months. I loved to see the world blanketed in snow, looking almost like the black-and-white movies my mom used to watch.

One Saturday, Rosemary invited me to go to the mall with her friend Fern. I initially said no. I had never met Fern and was unsure how we would get along based on what I knew about her. Besides, I knew Rosemary felt bad for me, and I did not want this to be her sole reason for inviting me places.

However, she was insistent, and after I remembered the little bookstore in the mall that I hadn't been to in ages, I relented somewhat reluctantly, despite the incentive of the bookstore. Three hours later, we were in the car, all bundled up in puffy coats, on our way to Ashton Heights Mall. We clambered out of the minivan to the sight of a mall all dolled up for Christmas, which was just a couple of weeks away. I had been so busy that the Christmas season had rolled around without my noticing.

We met Fern in the bookstore, a quaint little shop tucked away in a quiet corner of the bustling mall. Rosie introduced us, and I could tell that she would spend much of the day translating. Introductions had always been a little uncomfortable for me, but Fern seemed nice enough, although she had the intimidating appearance of someone who's used to getting her way.

After a while, Rosie and Fern started talking about school, and I wandered off among the tall shelves of books. I found a book on trees that I thought I might pick up before we left. I also found a book of Robert Frost poetry. I skimmed through, looking for the poem we read in school, the one that made me think so deeply into trees in the first place. For some reason, I was a little nervous, skimming through the cream-colored pages. Since the night of the failed experiment, I was a bit wary of this topic. I had halted all work on my project, and was thinking of a way to change course altogether. Eventually I found what I was looking for: *The Sound of Trees*. I read through the poem, surprised to find that it was longer than the excerpt that had been in our English textbook. I tore through the second stanza. One line in particular caught my attention: "I shall make the reckless choice/ Some day when they are in voice."

Was that what I had done? It was a reckless choice, absolutely. But what had prompted me to do that? Suddenly, the thoughts came back, a nasty snowstorm that swayed the trees almost to the breaking point. I shall make the reckless choice... My senses seemed to dull.

I distantly felt Rosemary tugging on my arm, asking if I was ready to move on to another store. The fluorescent lights seemed too white, too bright, too artificial. The advertisements covering every square foot of the glossy walls seemed far too colorful. I let Rosemary and Fern lead me out of the bookstore, only peripherally aware of my surroundings. I realized that my hands were moving, silently giving voice to the poem. I couldn't get it out of my head.

The sound of trees, I signed absentmindedly, my fingers going through the motions of the poem as I walked. Rosie, watching me out of the corner of her eye, froze. *Audrey!* She signed, grabbing my arm. Her excitement broke me out of the trance I had been in.

Confused, I replied. *It's a poem we read in school. It's about trees.*

She looked at Fern, her mouth wide open, and started laughing. Fern seemed just as confused as I was. Rosemary rapidly said something to her, and then began signing to me. *That's the poem! The one we were looking for at the library! All this time, you knew it!*

She slapped her palm to her forehead, grinning. *Why didn't I think to ask you?* She wondered, shaking her head, her brown wavy hair bobbing. *So what's it called?*

The Sound of Trees. It was in a book I found at the bookstore.

I didn't fully understand why this meant so much to her, but my sister took my hand and Fern's, and marched us right back to that bookstore. It was like the trees had been to me, I thought. It was just something she needed to know.

A word plastered on the wall caught my eye: *epiphany*. The Feast of the Epiphany was coming up, soon after Christmas, but the word has another meaning. It is often used to describe a revelation, like the one my sister had in the mall.

Thinking hard, I led them to the shelf where I had found the book, but it was gone. Puzzled, we all instinctively looked on the surrounding shelves, but it was nowhere to be found.

"You're sure it was here?" Fern asked me, and Rosemary translated.

I nodded vigorously. *Definitely.*

We scanned the bookstore. It was empty except for one tall young woman checking a book out, who looked vaguely familiar. She turned her head, and I saw lots of colored beads swinging in her hair, and suddenly I realized that it was Miss Strayer, Rosemary's violin instructor.

Rosemary quickly explained this to Fern, who nodded. Rosemary got a mischievous glint in her eye, and walked over to the checkout counter.

My sister said something to her, and Miss Strayer turned around with a surprised smile. They had a quick conversation, and Miss Strayer waved to Fern and me. Rosie asked something, pointing to the shopping bag in Miss Strayer's hand, and Miss Strayer opened it up, pulling out the book I had been looking at. I shared a knowing look with Fern. Rosemary nodded politely, and I knew that she was trying to figure out a way to ask to look through the book without overstepping.

I remembered something suddenly that would get my sister out of this potentially embarrassing situation, and so I tapped on her shoulder and signed something. *We have a book at home with the poem in it! We don't need this one.*

She nodded slowly, absorbing the information. She said something to Miss Strayer, who smiled and nodded, waving to us as Rosemary dragged us away.

What did you tell her? I asked.

Oh, I just said that my dad was waiting for us outside, and that we had to go, she said, repeating herself out loud for Fern.

I tilted my head at her. *You could've told her the truth.*

Rosie gave me a look I couldn't quite decipher. *That's not as fun,* she signed. *Also, I feel like we're on a mission or something, and I didn't want to have to explain it all.*

And so you lied?

And so I didn't tell her the entire story.

I was flustered. *But Dad isn't here!*

Audrey! Why is this so important?

Fern said something, and Rosemary

translated for me. *Let's go this way. There are cool stores over here.*

I looked at my sister, but she stared straight ahead of her. We started walking.

As we walked, just wandering the mall at this point, they told me about the poems they found, and about how they had already identified the one in Fern's folder. I had never really listened to Mom's poetry when she read it to us, but the Emily Dickinson one sounded familiar. We stopped at the food court after a while for a snack. Suddenly, I spotted Miss Strayer out of the corner of my eye, ordering at the Starbucks counter. I nudged Rosemary and Fern, frantically signing to them. Rosie had told her that we were leaving, and I didn't want to have to explain to Miss Strayer the whole poem predicament that we had been in. Oddly, Rosie's reaction didn't bother me as much now.

Silently and nervously laughing, we dove into the first store we came to, which happened to be a candy store. We decided to just splurge on some sugar instead of the only slightly-healthier options that the food court offered.

Later that night, I thought about what had happened. Sometimes my deepest, craziest thoughts happened late at night, so depending on how I was feeling, sometimes I would try to stay up late and other times, I would try to get to sleep as soon as physically possible.

Tonight though, I was not trying to do either. I simply had trouble sleeping, staring at the ceiling while my mind took me in circles. Why? I kept asking myself the question. Why was Rosemary so concerned about the poems? Why was I so concerned about the trees? Why was I so unusual? Why did Benjamin love me so much? Why did Mommy have to die? Why, why, why, why, why? Why was the universe splitting? And why did I feel like I was splitting with it?

I closed my eyes, silently willing my brain to stop, but as usual, it persisted in its stubborn ramblings. I thought again of Rosemary's expression at the mall, as though something of great importance had just been revealed to her.

Perhaps I was in need of an epiphany of some sort, as well.

24. swinging

WHEN AUDREY AND I were really little, Dad built a tire swing for us, out of a tire from our old car and a thick rope suspended from our tallest maple tree. In our five-year-old minds, nothing could be as exciting as our first swing on it. We would often spend hours at a time taking turns swinging on it. Dad had secured the thick rope to a tree branch high up in the tree, so you could swing really far. It felt like flying. My mom actually hired a professional photographer to take pictures of us on the swing in our little caps and gowns when we graduated kindergarten. But even more fun were the little moments that we would spend swinging, talking, swinging, laughing, or even just sitting quietly. One time I remember looking outside as a kid and seeing Dad pushing Mom on the swing. I called Audrey over and we stood there together, just watching them, feeling quiet and safe and happy. And lucky, I guess, although I only realize that in hindsight.

When we were ten, a wild March snowstorm pulled the tree down, snapping the rope and crushing the rubber tire swing. I still think about it sometimes, though.

A couple days after the mall, I was scheduled for another Latin tutoring session with Mrs. Perez. For some reason, I was thinking about the tire swing. It was childish, but I really missed it. Dad had said he would make another one, but with Mom's death so soon afterwards, it didn't seem right, I suppose.

I was still mulling over all that had occurred at the mall, and the small breakthrough we had made in our mystery. I have no idea why I had never thought to ask Audrey about the poem. But I guessed that maybe it was something I wanted to keep to myself. For all of my life I had shared every experience with her, and I suppose I wanted something to call my own. However, I had wanted to keep the violin to myself, and that didn't go so well. I wanted to keep a secret, but things rarely go as planned, like the trip to the mall, or the night of the concert.

I had tutoring right before orchestra again, so I arrived early, determined not to be late to orchestra again, especially after I suspected that Mr. Alden may have planted the notes. I couldn't think of why he would want to do such a thing, but still he seemed the most likely suspect, and so I would try not to upset him. Again.

So I was waiting outside Mrs. Perez's classroom door again, but this time it was slightly ajar. I was so deep in thought that I didn't notice at first that Mrs. Perez was crying. They were the kind of quietly violent sobs that don't make a lot of noise, but make a whole lot of tears.

I couldn't make out words, but after a little while, she began crying harder. I realized then that I should not be listening, whether or not she was the one late for tutoring, and so I moved further down the hallway and tried to tune out the hiccups coming from the classroom door, pulling out a math worksheet I had been working on for homework. I worked quietly for a while, trying to drown out the sounds that I couldn't help hearing.

She soon seemed to settle down, but it was

still a little while before she came to the door and noticed me. It took me by surprise when I looked up and found her looking down at me from the doorway.

"Oh! I didn't see you there!" I exclaimed as I looked up at her. She was smiling, and unless I hadn't heard her, I wouldn't have been able to tell that she had been crying. She escorted me into the room, and we proceeded with the lesson. In between learning verbs and conjugations and vocabulary, I thought about the dream I had, with the chess pawns and the mirror. Mrs. Perez had been there, and I wondered if I had only dreamed about her because I had had a Latin lesson that day, or if it was because of something else.

I felt like we were on the tire swing. We were swinging between a lot of things, I thought. We would find a new clue, and then a new mystery, and then a new clue, and then a new mystery. Back and forth, back and forth, back and forth. The setting would change, but the mystery remained the same, with the uncertainty just as real and just as frightening. I wondered if that was all that life was, in the end. You spend your life trying to solve mysteries, and in the end, a mystery solves you. But I didn't think so.

I thought about my parents, sitting outside on the tire swing. Sometimes, you just have to let the mysteries be. I decided that I would stop trying to play detective. It was childish, after all. I was just a little kid trying to be Sherlock Holmes. But this was high school. Things didn't work out that way.

25. secreTs

ONE DAY IN MID-DECEMBER, I decided to go for a walk, partially in an attempt to clear my mind, partially to get out of the house, and partially to explore. I had a feeling that maybe it was an adventurous sort of day.

It was cold, but no colder than usual, and I went out with the customary coat, hat, scarf, gloves, and boots that the New England winters require. Rosie was at Fern's house and Dad was working, so I went alone. Winter was my favorite season. The leaves lost their vibrancy and the world was full of just a few simple colors. I liked it that way.

When I was about nine, I tried to run away on a day like this. I had always loved being by myself outdoors. It was not exactly like being alone, but not like being with other people, either. The house had been particularly crowded that day, and I needed to get away from it all. When my dad tells the story, he makes it seem like I just walked out on a whim and tried to run away. But in reality, I knew what I was doing. I never did anything on a whim; I had a plan. I didn't intend to be away very long; in fact, I had hoped to be back before anyone realized I had left. But I took a wrong turn, and I got lost. When Dad and Mom realized I was gone, a search party was organized, and I was quickly marched back home. After that incident, I was given a small spiral-bound pad of paper to carry around whenever I was by myself, in case I had to communicate with anyone who couldn't sign. That was one of the best things about my parents - they never forbade me to do anything, but they made sure I would do it responsibly.

And so I trudged along the sidewalk, fingering the little spiral-bound pad, the same one from five years ago. I had never needed it, and hoped I never would.

I didn't really think about much while I walked, just kind of zoned out and went for a stroll. After a while I wasn't really watching where I was going. While I was peripherally monitoring when to look both ways before crossing a street, I wasn't exactly registering which streets I was crossing.

After a while, it began to snow. I looked up, and the fluffy clouds of a few hours ago had morphed into a swirling mass of dark snow clouds. I shivered, looked around, and turned in the general direction of home. After a few minutes, the snow was really coming down, and it was hard to see the path. I stopped to consider my options. I could go home, which could take hours in this weather, or I could stop along the way.

I remembered that Miss Strayer lived around here. I didn't want to drop in without any warning, but I didn't really have a choice. Dad would be worried if I wasn't home soon, and walking all the way home would certainly take longer than I was prepared for. I set off through the increasingly snow-blanketed streets, looking up at the sky when I wasn't making sure I didn't trip on something beneath the thickening layer of snow. The trees were black silhouettes against the murky sky. I wondered if the root systems were still active when the tree was dormant. I wondered again, for the first time since the night of the experiment, why a tree would sabotage another. I had been unable to find an answer to that question, which still nagged at the back of my mind. Were they partial to trees of the same species, or closely related ones? Was there family loyalty among trees? Something in me hoped that that was true, though I wasn't sure why.

I made it to Miss Strayer's house in a few minutes, and after a brief hesitation, knocked on the door. I said a quick prayer that she would be home, fingering the rosary in my pocket. I rarely prayed, but I was rarely in a situation like this. My mother had always kept a rosary in her pocket, though I seldom saw her take it out. I guess she thought it protected her anyway. I hadn't prayed much since she died. I don't know what my sister thought, but when God let my mother die, I didn't find much value in prayer anymore.

I mused on how strange it was that it was now that I thought to pray, not when I was crumpled on the floor the night of the concert. As I thought about how weird that was, I realized that whatever I would have prayed for as I sat on my bedroom floor, crying into the fur of the cat I most certainly didn't deserve - those prayers were answered.

A glint from the stained glass windows distracted me from my thoughts, thoughts that always got far too dark, far too quickly. I was grateful for the interruption.

The heavy wooden door creaked as Miss Strayer pulled it open. She tilted her head to the side, confused. She said something out loud, and then slapped a hand to her mouth, as though she had said something she shouldn't have. I knew that she had forgotten that I couldn't hear. Not having thought this problem through yet, I finally dug through my coat pocket for the pad of paper, which I was now glad to have remembered. I scrawled a quick message on it, holding it up with a gloved hand for her to see. *It's me, Audrey. Rosemary Cooper's sister. Could I come in for a little while? I got stuck in the storm.*

Her dark eyes widened as she read my message. She nodded vigorously, beckoning for me to enter. The foyer of her little house was still dappled with color from the stained-glass windows bordering the front door, even in such bleak weather. She held up one finger as I stepped in, signaling for me to wait. I stood in the warm foyer, soaking in the warmth while also very aware of all the snow dripping off me onto the hardwood floor. I tried to keep the melting snow contained, but to no avail.

Miss Strayer found me a few minutes later, looking sheepishly at the puddle of water growing around my boots. She was carrying a towel, a small whiteboard, and a cup of coffee.

She handed me the towel, and scribbled something on the whiteboard. *Stay as long as you need to. Do you want me to call your dad? I'll go grab the telephone.*

That hadn't occurred to me, strangely enough. As usual, I was more occupied with thoughts of trees, and cats, and God, instead of the more practical things. I nodded. She went into another room, coming back a couple moments later with a phone. She scribbled something else on the whiteboard. *Tell me what to say.*

This struck me as one of those statements that always seemed large and unapproachable and unanswerable, though I knew that wasn't Miss Strayer's intent.

I considered for a moment, before wiping the board clean and writing on it. *Tell him that I'm fine, but I got stuck in the storm. If he could pick me up, that would be great.*

She nodded, and dialed a number. She held the phone to her ear and talked, her face mirroring the tone of the conversation. I know that a lot of deaf people can read lips, and sometimes I wish I could, but I never was able to learn how. My dad says that he and Mom tried to teach me, but it was too late, and the "prime learning window" had passed. At some point, I had done some research into that phrase, since it was one that he used whenever he brought up the topic, as though he had read it in a textbook. I found it in a book once, about child development. Apparently, there are certain skills that can easily be learned at a certain age, such as talking, and walking, and, apparently, lip reading. If you wait until this window passes, learning the particular skill is extremely difficult.

I was a little disappointed in myself. Being able to read lips would make things a lot easier, even if I still couldn't speak. I think I would be okay with not being able to speak. I don't often have a lot to say. I suspected that it would make everything easier, though. Easier to communicate, easier to go to school, easier to understand. Easier to be understood.

Miss Strayer got off the phone a few moments later, and picked up the whiteboard. *He said that he is on his way to pick up Rosemary from a friend's, and will be by to pick you up in about half an hour.*

175

I nodded, and she wiped the board clean. *So we have a half hour. Here, have some coffee.* She handed me the mug. I had never tried coffee before, but I had tried coffee ice cream once, so I figured it couldn't be that much different. I took a tentative sip, and found that it was full of cream and sugar and cinnamon, and that it was delicious. I smiled, and gave her a thumbs up. She grinned, and turned back to the whiteboard. *Take your time. But when you're done, what do you say we try out those musical abilities of yours a bit more?*

I smiled and nodded. We went down the still-cluttered hallway into the music room. The blinds were wide open, and we had a magnificent view of the snow falling through the giant picture window. It gave me the feeling of being closed in, but in a good way.

Miss Strayer sat down at the piano, and beckoned me to sit down next to her. She began to play, her hands moving so rapidly that they were blurring before my eyes. After a while, my eyes began to wander as I took in the music. I looked out the window, where the snow was falling more slowly now, and my eyes once again fell on the grainy photo hanging on the wall in front of me. It looked old, and I wondered why she kept it hanging if it was so blurry and smudged. I must have been looking at it for a while, for I felt the music stop suddenly. I looked over at Miss Strayer, who was looking at the photo with me. She pulled the whiteboard out from where it sat on the piano, scribbling something on it. *That was my mom.*

I nodded politely. *I'm sorry.*

She took the marker from me. She opened her mouth to say something, closed it, picked up the marker to write something down, and snapped the cap on it.

I turned my eyes back to the piano keyboard, but I kept thinking about the picture.

She turned back to the piano, taking my hands and placing them on the keys. She motioned to me in a *go ahead* sort of way, and, surprised, I tentatively pressed down on them. I could feel the vibrations traveling through my fingers and up my arms, all throughout my body. Miss Strayer smiled, and put my fingers on specific keys, building a chord. I pressed down on the keys, finding the vibrations more. . . agreeable this time, like they were working together.

Miss Strayer stood up, and fished out a violin from the conglomeration of instruments on the floor. She began to play, and our two melodies wove together. I wondered if this was what the concert had been like. After a while, Miss Strayer evidently heard something, and put down the violin. She got up and left the room, and a few minutes later, Rosemary and Dad walked in the room. Rosemary waved. *Quite an adventure you got yourself into, huh?* She asked with a lopsided grin.

I shrugged. *More of an adventure than you had, I would guess.*

She opened her mouth in feigned shock. *Oh, I wouldn't bet on it.*

I looked up at the adults, who were talking rapidly. I signed to Rosemary, *What are they saying?*

Grown-up stuff. The weather, and payment for music lessons and stuff.

Oh. Ok. I watched them for a while. It was like a secret language that everyone knew but me. Suddenly, I realized that sign language must seem like a secret language to people like Miss Strayer. I had never thought of it that way before.

26. pAssengers

IT ALWAYS SURPRISES ME to see someone out in public for the first time. When Audrey and I went to the mall with Fern, I was shocked by how different she acted when she wasn't in a school environment. She carried herself differently, I thought, and she laughed more. I wondered if I acted any differently when I was in school.

Seeing Miss Strayer at the mall was just as odd. Instead of being my violin teacher, she was a shopper, almost a stranger, even. It's funny how people you think you know well can be so different when you change the setting. It's like we're all characters in a book, but the time and place of the book keeps changing, and we're never sure how we'll react.

As we drove Audrey home after her accidental expedition into the snowstorm, I was sitting in the front passenger seat. She and I had made an agreement two years ago when we graduated to the front seat. On Mondays, Wednesdays, and Fridays, I got to sit in the passenger seat while she sat in the back, and on Tuesdays, Thursdays, and Saturdays, she got to take shotgun. On Sundays, we both sat in the back. As it was a Wednesday, I was up front with Dad.

It had always struck me as a little odd how the seat next to the driver's seat was always called the "passenger" seat. I had never ridden in a taxi before, but in the movies, the passengers always sat in the back. When we went for road trips, the passenger seat became the copilot's seat. Whoever was sitting up front was always in charge of the map. When you're sitting in the back, you don't have any control of where you go. I think that a fairly important element of being a passenger is putting your transportation in someone else's hands.

As we were pulling out of Miss Strayer's street, I saw a familiar figure sitting in a car on the street parallel to Miss Strayer's. As I looked closer, I saw that it was Mrs. Perez. I tilted my head to the side in surprise. Dad noticed. "Who's that?" he asked.

"Just one of my teachers."

He slowed down. "You want to go say hello?"

I shook my head vehemently. I didn't want to have to see her out of her element like this. Something inside my head said that interactions with teachers should only happen within the confines of school, though I knew that was childish. I thought about Miss Strayer in the bookstore. That had gone rather well, although Miss Strayer was so very different from Mrs. Perez. However, I was curious about what I had overheard in the classroom, and I leaned forward in my seat to get a better look, praying that she wouldn't look out the window and see me. She appeared to be just sitting, surveying the neighborhood.

As though reading my thoughts, Dad looked over to her car. "She looks lost," he said.

I shrugged. "Maybe she's just waiting for someone?"

"I'll pull over and ask if she needs help."

I thought about protesting, but didn't want to seem like I didn't want to help her. Considering that she may or may not realize that I overheard her from the hallway before my tutoring session, I didn't want her to think that I had been following her, or something similarly suspicious. The thought had occurred to me, one night when I couldn't sleep, and my thoughts tended to go a little wild. I knew I would never really follow her around, especially since my decision to drop the whole thing. But still, a part of me was desperate for just this kind of adventure.

Either way, Dad was attempting a three-point-turn to save Mrs. Perez from whatever conundrum she happened to be in.

He pulled up next to her car, facing the opposite direction so that he could talk to her. He rolled down his window, but she didn't seem to have noticed us yet. She sat with her hands on the steering wheel and her head facing downwards. I looked behind me at Audrey.

She was watching Mrs. Perez intently, a puzzled look on her face.

After an awkward few moments that felt much longer, Mrs. Perez finally noticed the car pulled up next to hers. She quickly rolled down her window. "Can I help you?" she asked.

Dad shook his head. "We were just

wondering if you needed directions or something."

She smiled wanly. "No, thank you." She suddenly noticed me. "Is that you, Rosemary?" she asked with a smile.

I nodded and waved. "Hi, Mrs. Perez."

Dad took the opportunity to make a new friend, as usual. "I'm Ralph Cooper, Rosemary's dad."

She nodded curtly. "Cornelia Perez. Nice to meet you. Your Rosemary's one of my brightest students."

I was surprised. Bright students generally did not need tutoring.

Dad glanced over at me. "Thank you," he said with a smile in my direction. "Well, I suppose we should be going. It was lovely making your acquaintance." With a wave, Dad drove off. He often lapsed into the vernacular of the eighteenth century, which was probably one of the side effects of being a history professor.

As we drove off, I thought about what we'd seen. Though Mrs. Perez sat in the driver's seat, she sure didn't look like she knew where she was going.

27. arguments

AS WE SAT IN THE CAR while Dad and Rosemary talked with Mrs. Perez, I couldn't stop thinking that I'd seen her somewhere. I scanned my memory for any time I might have run into her. It was funny, how memory works, how you can get so close to a memory without really remembering it. I couldn't think of any occasion in which I might have seen her, especially since I'd never been to Rosemary's school before.

After a few moments of chatting, we pulled away, turned around with a clumsily executed seven-point-turn, and set off for home.

It was still snowing, but the storm had become less intense, the flakes falling slowly, peacefully, quietly now. It had lost all of its frightening splendor, and I wished it would stop. Turning my eyes away from the window, I watched Rosie and Dad argue lightheartedly in the front seat.

When we got home, Rosemary beckoned me into her bedroom. She plopped down on her bed, and I sat on the thick carpet. Rosie looked excited, a mischievous glint in her green eyes. She began signing rapidly. *Did you notice anything weird about how Mrs. Perez was just sitting in the car like that?*

I thought for a moment. *A little. She didn't look lost. And Rosie. . .I thought I recognized her from somewhere. Is there anywhere I might have seen her?*

She tilted her head to the side and paused. *Not that I can think of.*

I couldn't think of anywhere, either. I really feel like I've seen her before, though.

The mystery deepens, she said with a grin. After a brief hesitation, she told me about what she had overheard in Mrs. Perez's classroom while waiting for her tutoring session. About how the teacher had been screaming at someone over the phone, and then later, crying.

Do you think she's up to something?

Rosie shrugged, suppressing a guilty smile.

Is it bad that I kind of hope she is? I need some adventure.

I didn't know. *What do you suspect she's doing?*

She looked out the window for a moment. *I'm not sure. I keep thinking that she could be in trouble, too. Maybe she's not causing it. Maybe she needs help.* She looked me in the eye. *I told myself I was going to drop all this. But I think I'm changing my mind. Do you think I'm being ridiculous?*

I'm not sure. I think it could definitely be nothing, but it could be something important. You're not a detective though, Rosie. She might not want you prying into her business like this.

She nodded vigorously. *I know. I just don't know what to do.*

The conversation died off, and we both sat for a while, just watching the snow fall in the front yard. After a little while, she turned back to me. *So,* she signed, *what did you do at Miss Strayer's? Did she do any more music stuff with you?*

I nodded. I told her about the coffee, and how she let me play the piano, and about the little whiteboard.

Wow, Aud. That's awesome. She seemed genuinely impressed, and I was confused. *What is?*

*Just. . .all of it. How you just managed to talk to her. Do you ever. . .*she trailed off, unsure of what to say.

What?

Do you ever get mad? About how you can't talk to people? And how other people can't understand you when you sign?

I shrugged. *Sometimes. But I don't have a lot to say.*

She shook her head. *You have so much to say. You just don't choose to say it.*

I thought about what she meant. I had lots of thoughts in my head, sure, but I couldn't possibly translate them all to words, could I? I had never understood how people were able to sustain conversations for hours at a time, without ever once stopping to think. *Maybe I do. But I don't know how to say it all.*

Nobody does, Audrey. Nobody has it all figured out. Did you think that everyone knew exactly what to say, all the time?

I shrugged. I guess I had.

We don't. I never know the right thing to say. Dad never knows the right thing to say. Mom never knew the right thing to say.

Yes she did. She wrote poetry. That's like, the

ultimate way to say something.

Did you know that some of her poems took her months to write? That's what poetry is. It's just trying to find the right words. It's the whole process just laid out on paper.

Really? Rosemary nodded. I thought about Mommy, writing poetry, holding Rosemary and me as babies. She always said we did all the same things, despite our differences. There's a picture hanging in our living room of Mommy holding both Rosemary and me in an easy chair. It's my favorite photo. I love it because it was taken before anyone realized I was deaf. In that picture, Rosie and I are the same. Parallel lines.

Suddenly something clicked in my brain, like two puzzle pieces sliding together. *Rosie!* I signed frantically.

She evidently thought I was continuing the previous conversation, because her eyes softened. *It's okay, Aud -* she began, but I cut her off, shaking my head wildly, grabbing her arm. *Rosie! The picture! Miss Strayer has a picture of Mrs. Perez hanging on her wall!*

She stood up. *What?*

Yes! It's a really blurry, grainy picture of a lady holding a baby, and they're not smiling, and I always thought it was weird because it's kind of a bad picture to hang up. But Mrs. Perez is the woman holding the baby!

Rosemary started jumping up and down. *Wait, wait, wait!* she said. It was hard to follow her signing with her jumping like that. *I know that picture! Are they standing outside, under a tree, in the fall? And it's kind of crooked, like the camera wasn't straight?* Her eyes were wide, and her hands were fidgeting with the hem of her sweatshirt. I nodded.

That picture is on Mrs. Perez's desk at school! I just remembered that! Wait - you said it's hanging up in Miss Strayer's house?

Yes - right across from the piano. Next to the window, in the corner.

She shook her head. *How did I never notice that before?* Her eyes widened and she slapped a hand to her forehead. *So Mrs. Perez is Miss Strayer's MOTHER?*

I shrugged. *It's definitely her in the picture.* Suddenly, my eyes widened as I remembered something. *Wait. Rosemary.* I signed seriously. She stopped her crazed jumping and looked intently at me. *What?*

When I was at Miss Strayer's place today, she saw me looking at the picture. She said it was her mom. Past tense. But it was definitely Mrs. Perez.

So Miss Strayer thinks her mom is dead? Or . . .something like that?

I shrugged. We both stopped for a moment to process that. The silence was almost tangible, and I knew we were both thinking about Mom.

Rosemary finally looked at me. *You're sure it's her?*

I nodded. *Almost positive.*

Audrey, she signed, *do you know what this means?*

I noticed her mischievous expression, and got a little nervous all of a sudden. I shook my head slowly, hesitantly.

We have to reunite them! Her hands moved in wild, exaggerated movements, the signing equivalent of yelling at me.

I just looked at her. *Rosemary. . .*

She tilted her head to the side. *What's wrong?*

I didn't know how to articulate what I was thinking. Rosemary was wrong; I didn't have much to say, and when I thought of something, I didn't know how to say it. *I just. . .I don't know. How do you know they want to be reunited?*

She looked at me in disbelief. *Audrey. If. . .* she paused, and swallowed hard. *If Mom came back. .*

.

I nodded. *I know. But that's different.*

No, it isn't!

I stared at her. *Rosie, you weren't there. Miss Strayer doesn't want to see her mom.*

I watched her take this information in. She didn't want to, I knew, but it was something she had to understand. She swallowed hard again, and her eyes hardened a bit, like she was trying not to cry.

Miss Strayer had almost looked angry as she talked about her mom. The last thing I wanted was to get caught up in that. I didn't want to know any more about the situation than I already did. Part of me was afraid, I think, that I would discover something that would make me angry at my own mother, and I didn't think I could handle that.

28. letting go (gravitY)

MY DAD NEVER raked leaves. He believed that dead leaves were a natural fertilizer, and were good for the grass. So he let them fall, and let them be. We had a neighbor who always went out with her leaf blower whenever a handful of leaves fell, and Mommy used to laugh and laugh and laugh. I think she felt bad for her, though. All that work, and nature still won.

Anyway, when Mom was still here, we used to go sit outside in the fall, all together as a family. We each had our own camping chairs, and we would set up camp somewhere in our big backyard. Sometimes we would talk, sometimes Audrey and I would run around or play with a Frisbee, but my favorite times were when we would each bring out a book or an activity to do by ourselves. It was peaceful, and quiet, and. . . real. I would bring one of my fantasy books, Audrey would bring a science book, and Dad would do the crossword puzzle from the morning's newspaper. Mommy's activities varied. Sometimes she would knit, or crochet, sometimes she'd read a poetry book, or a nonfiction book, or a novel, or the news. Sometimes she'd bring out her notebook and write poems. Occasionally she'd read a line out loud, and we would all chime in with what we thought the next line should be. Somewhere, Dad has the notebook where Mom wrote down these "poem chains," as she liked to call them, miscellaneous lines of text that we all contributed to. They were often chaotic, and asymmetrical, and crazy, just like we were.

No matter what we chose to do, we would occasionally stop, and just watch the leaves fall. It sounds boring, I know, but in a way it was like fishing; it's quiet, and you just sit there doing nothing, but something always brings you back to it. And all year round, you would see the leaves in the yard. In the spring, they were beginning to decay under the melting snow, and although it doesn't sound at all spring-like, to us it was just another sign of new life. In the summer, they got chopped up in the lawn mower, and began to fertilize the new grass. In the fall, new leaves fell, and all through the winter, there was a layer of dead leaves decaying beneath the snow.

There is a poem that my mom wrote about falling leaves. It's not just your typical tree poem; she goes into the science of what makes the leaves fall and ties it all together with a beautiful woven pattern of words. It's my favorite poem of hers.

When leaves fall, she told me, it's not just gravity that pulls them down. The tree has to expend its energy; it has to work to destroy the molecules that bind the leaf to the branch. The tree has to choose to let them fall.

When Audrey told me about Miss Strayer and her mom, I got really angry. Miss Strayer had no right to hate her own mother. I hated the fact that my mother, my wonderful mother who I loved with everything I had, had died in a car accident, leaving a gaping, mother-shaped hole in our family, while Miss Strayer's mother lived a decent life in the same town as a daughter who hated her and thought she was dead. It was magnificently unfair.

My mother died four years ago, but there were still leaves I wasn't ready to let go of yet.

A few days after my conversation with Audrey, I sat alone in the school library during lunch. The cafeteria had been unusually noisy and I retreated to the library to study for my history test next period. I had only memorized five key terms when I saw a figure scrambling into the library out of the corner of my eye.

I jerked my head up, and saw Fern Reynolds walking towards my table. I hadn't seen much of her after the day at the mall. She was clingy with her group during school, but often said hi to me when I passed her in the hallway. I was surprised to see her in the library.

"Rosemary!" she exclaimed, at a volume that would have given a librarian a heart attack, if we had had a school librarian.

"What?"

"New development. C'mere!" I got up, and followed her over to a shelf near the back of the library. She turned to face me. "I was here yesterday, studying, and all of a sudden I realized that we found the poems, but not here. I checked the poetry section again, and couldn't find the Frost one. But then I realized that if it was a student, they would probably have found it in a textbook! So I dug around a bit, and found this."

She pulled out an old English textbook, skimmed over until she found the page she was looking for, in the back. She flipped the book around and shoved it at me. Surprised, I took it and began to read. There were two poems on the page. One was "The Brain is Wider than the Sky" by Emily Dickinson, and the other was "The Sound of Trees" by Robert Frost.

But more importantly, there was a pink sticky note stuck to the bottom of the page. The handwriting was small, lightly scrawled in pencil. It was a one-word message. "Sorry," it said. I squinted to read the signature at the bottom of the note, which was small and messy. It read "Miranda." The neon sticky note was in stark contrast with the nervous handwriting. I stared at it for a moment.

My eyes wide, I looked up at Fern, who jumped up and down a little bit in her boots. She was proud of herself, I could tell, and she looked at me with her eyebrows raised in expectation.

"Who's Miranda?" I asked.

"Unfortunately, I have no idea. But we're going to find out."

"Let's check the student directory, and then maybe the yearbooks. I bet they have them all archived somewhere."

Her face lit up, and I could tell that she hadn't thought of that.

The directory was a dead end, with no Mirandas, but we still had all the yearbooks to go through.

We dug around a bit, and eventually found the yearbooks at the back of the library. They had them going back thirty years, and we checked the senior page of all of them. There were no Mirandas. After going back through all the yearbooks, we slumped on the floor. "It's like whoever set this up doesn't want anyone to discover it." I said.

She nodded. "But they keep giving clues."

"Right. I guess every detective must have felt like this, though. There's no such thing as an easy mystery."

She pointed at me with one blue fingernail. "True."

She tilted her head at me so the bun on the top of her head slumped to the side. "Is that what we are? Detectives?"

I laughed. "All this time, I've been picturing myself as Sherlock Holmes."

She held up her hands with her index fingers and thumbs extended to make a frame.

"Sherlock Rosemary and the Mystery of the High School Orchestra."

I laughed again. "Wouldn't it be Rosemary Holmes, though? Sherlock's his first name, Holmes is his last."

She tilted her head again. "Really?" I giggled as she went on. "I always thought it was a title, like 'doctor' or 'professor.' Like a pro detective somehow gains the title of 'sherlock.'"

I was practically rolling on the library floor at this point. "The two esteemed sherlocks, Rosemary Cooper and Fern Reynolds, finally crack the case of the Robert Frost poem."

Now she laughed. For some reason, I decided to tell her about Miss Strayer and Mrs. Perez. I needed a second opinion; I wanted someone to agree with me. After I explained the situation and swore her to secrecy, she sighed. "That's a tough one," she said. "Did you know that my parents are divorced?"

I shook my head, suddenly realizing how little I knew about her. And how different our childhoods must have been. "I'm sorry." After a moment, I asked, "Did you know that my mom's dead?"

Her eyes widened. "No, I had no idea. I'm

so sorry, that must be hard."

I nodded, marveling at this girl in front of me, head of the popular crowd, makeup expert, queen of the shiny hair, but also the girl who read poetry, who searched through libraries for answers, who was a surprisingly genuine friend. She was as much of an enigma as the mystery we were trying to solve.

"Hm." she said, deep in thought. "So your sister said that your violin teacher doesn't want to meet her mom."

"Not exactly. She just said she seemed angry when she talked about her."

"Ok. She's angry at her mom, so Audrey doesn't want to mess with it."

"Yeah."

"But you're thinking about your mom, and if she was still alive, right? So you want to reunite them so that Mrs. Perez doesn't die before Miss Strayer can see her again."

"Right." How had she known that? I hadn't mentioned my conversation with Audrey about Mommy.

The bell rang, startling us out of our thoughts. We scrambled to get our books and things, and hurried off to class.

The rest of the day, I thought about our conversation. I thought about leaves, and how you had to choose what grudges, what thoughts, what memories you hold on to, and which ones you let go of. I wasn't ready to let go of my anger at the driver who had killed Mom, and I didn't think I ever would. I had let go of my frustration at Audrey when she said she didn't want to mess with the mystery. But as I thought about what Fern had said, I realized that maybe Miss Strayer shouldn't let go of this. Maybe those leaves weren't meant to fall just yet.

29. procrastinating

I BEGAN MOST SUNDAY evenings trying to convince my sister to do her homework. She always waited until the last minute, and this caused me no end of anguish. Waiting even a few hours to do a task stressed me out, and I didn't like watching Rosemary frantically finish her assignments late Sunday night.

All my life, I had never been a procrastinator. When someone asked me to get something done, it got done. As soon as possible. I would watch Rosemary get distracted, put things off, wait until the last minute. She would frantically put a project together, finish a paper, and practice her music, all at the same time. I had never understood how a person could operate like that.

However, my school project had been assigned two months ago, and I still had not even touched half of it. Literature was a field I was slightly afraid of, a fact that I was not quite ready to admit. Or maybe I was afraid of the project itself.

Even with the recent hullabaloo with the poems at Rosie's school, I still didn't really understand poetry. I understood why Rosemary liked it so much, but I didn't share her enthusiasm. I didn't understand language the way that everyone else did.

One Saturday, I was sitting in my room, drawing a tree, its roots splaying out under the ground, thinking about how I was going to manage finishing this project. Benjamin wandered in my room, his long bushy tail swishing. I sat up, and he came over to me, settling comfortably in my lap.

For the millionth time, I tried to think of a way to incorporate the poem about the sound of trees. I was fascinated by it, but I couldn't even begin to put my fascination into words. It seemed a huge and unapproachable task.

I stroked Benjamin's head as he purred. I had managed to avoid thinking about my project due to what had happened on the night of the concert, but a part of me knew that I had to finish it. Not only for the grade, but for me.

I wanted to use *the Sound of Trees*, but I didn't know how to approach it. How could I even begin to analyze a poem with the word "sound" in the title? English had always been so difficult for me that I dreaded the idea of looking for a new piece of literature. I was procrastinating.

Procrastinate. It was an odd word, I thought. A quick dictionary search told me that the word came from Latin. Specifically, it came from the Latin word *crastinus*, meaning "belonging to tomorrow." That sounded rather nice, I thought. It almost gave the word a more positive connotation. It didn't, however, address the unrest inside me as I thought about all the things I should be doing, but wasn't. I was still afraid of those things.

30. miranda (liBrary)

ALL THE NEXT DAY I kept thinking about Miranda. I wondered who she was, and where she was, and what she was sorry for. Above all, I wondered why she wrote the notes. Why did she feel the need to hide her messages so obscurely? I wondered if she was only doing it for fun, but I didn't think so. There was a seriousness with which she wrote "sorry" that made me think it was far deeper than we had anticipated. Of course, it could be my imagination, but how could I know? Perhaps it was nothing more than a scavenger hunt for her friends. But if that was the case, why would the notes still be there? Clearly, the notes were not intended for Fern or me, but then who were they intended for? Was it possible that the original recipients never received them? My brain went around and around in circles all day, and I began to understand how my sister felt when she got lost in her thoughts.

The next day, a Saturday, was another quiet snowstorm day, the first one we'd had since Audrey went on her accidental adventure. We were yet again stuck inside, which always felt odd, even during the times of year where we rarely went anywhere anyway. But maybe we weren't as stuck as I thought. Audrey had certainly found a way around that.

Dad believed that Audrey and I were spending too much time alone. He had some errands to run, and offered to drop the two of us off at the local coffee shop, so we could get some homework done. Reluctantly I agreed, even though I would have preferred to stay home and watch it snow. Even I admitted that we hadn't been out anywhere besides school in a while.

Audrey and I packed up our books and ten minutes later, we were bundled up and piled into the minivan. Dad dropped us off at Ashton Coffee Roasters, and we quickly found a table and settled down in comfy pillow chairs by the window.

Audrey ordered a small coffee and a chocolate chip muffin. She'd been drinking coffee ever since she tried it at Miss Strayer's. I had tried it a few times, but ended up spitting it out in the sink when no one was looking.

After some deliberation, I got hot chocolate with whipped cream and a cinnamon roll.

Although the food was marvelous, my favorite thing about Ashton Coffee was the mini used bookstore. It was small enough that it never had anything you were looking for, but big enough that you could always find something you liked.

After I returned with our snacks, I sat down in the green easy chair that was pulled up to the multicolored table, under a low-hanging string of twinkling Christmas lights. Audrey had pulled out two textbooks, both of which were bigger than any of my school books. She had her nose buried in one, slouched down in her chair, her hair splayed out around her head, with the other book open on the table. I set my tote bag down on the limited table space still available, and pulled out a notebook.

Almost every table surrounding us was full, and the shop was full of color and small talk and laughter. It was an open-concept building, with the kitchen in full view of the customers. Underneath the twinkle lights, people chatted and giggled and gestured to one another. The baristas and cooks bustled around, and a few people sat on the couches near the bookshelves. It was full of a loud, chaotic sort of peace.

I couldn't really focus on my homework with all that was happening around us, so after a while, I got up to browse the bookshelves. I signed to Audrey where I was going, and she barely looked up. She was fully absorbed in her reading. Dad always told me to stay with her when we were out together, but I trusted her. Besides, she always had her pad of paper with her, and I wouldn't be far away.

The shelves were pretty close to the checkout counter, and I politely smiled at the barista as I passed. He was young, probably college age or older, and had the kind of face that a lot of the girls at school would swoon over. I stopped by the bookshelves, and ran my fingers over the spines. A lot of the books looked really old, and were almost falling apart. Those were my favorites. I flipped through the titles, finding a lot of obscure nonfiction, but with a couple novels in the mix. I finally settled on a battered copy of <u>Emma</u> by Jane Austen, which I had never read, and settled into one of the cloth-covered, patched-up couches in the corner. I glanced over at Audrey from time to time, but she was always in the same position I had left her in - hunched over her textbooks, occasionally looking up to glance out the window, which looked over the highway, and further away, the mountains.

About halfway through the first chapter of Emma, a familiar name caught my attention. The young barista had gotten on the phone, and was rapidly speaking to whoever was on the other end. I was just close enough to hear the murmur of whoever it was that was on the other end, but couldn't make out what they were saying. After a long pause, the barista began talking again. "I don't know," he said, and paused again. "Miranda, do you really think-?" He abruptly cut off, and I whipped my head up. *Miranda!* Of course, there were probably dozens of Mirandas in the area. Maybe five in Ashton Heights, a couple hundred in the state perhaps, but even so, the odds of my discovering two different Mirandas in such a short time period were quite small.

I listened closer, keeping my nose buried in the book, turning the pages every once in a while. I never knew how good of an eavesdropper I could be. I guess I had never had the opportunity to, before this year.

The conversation evidently became more serious, because Barista's voice dropped. "No, I can't come." Pause. "Mira, you know why." Long pause. "Do you think maybe she's wrong? I mean, you didn't even finish-" Pause. "Look, I really can't. I gotta go. I'll call you." Pause. "Okay, talk to you later." Pause. "Yeah, you too. Ok, love ya, bye."

I thought hard. *Miranda.* I glanced back at the barista, who was working hard to make a complicated-looking beverage. I tried my best to guess how old he was. Maybe twenty-five? If Miranda was his girlfriend, or friend, or something, then she was probably around the same age. I did a quick calculation in my head. If it was the same Miranda, then she would have graduated from St. Michael's about seven years ago. I flipped a page in Emma, though I couldn't have concentrated on the book even if I had been trying to.

Fern and I had looked through the yearbooks of the past twenty years. If she had graduated, we would have seen her name. There were no Mirandas, Miras, Randys, or Andys. We had checked every possible nickname for Miranda. We had even checked the faculty pages, though we doubted that a teacher would go to all that trouble.

A lightbulb went off in my head suddenly. *"You didn't even finish,"* the barista had told her. What if she hadn't graduated? We hadn't checked the other grades. Why hadn't we thought of that? After a while, I closed my book with a louder *snap* than I intended, and stood up. I brought the book over to the table, having decided that I would buy it. It was old, and the cover was half-falling off, but I fantasized that perhaps it was an early edition. Perhaps it was even a marvelously well-preserved first edition. I closed my eyes and pictured Jane Austen herself running her fingers over the cover of this very book.

Turning my mind back to the task at hand, I went back to the table, and tapped Audrey's shoulder. She seemed slightly annoyed at the disturbance, but ever since the day at the mall, she was in on the mystery, and I had to keep her updated. I rapidly related all that I'd heard, and watched her react. She didn't seem as excited about it as I was, which I found slightly irritating. Certainly her life was not so very interesting that she didn't long for some form of adventure. Her eyes widened as I related my theory, that she had indeed gone to St. Michael's, but hadn't graduated. The barista, I explained, must be her boyfriend.

After I had finished explaining, Audrey sighed. *Wow,* she said, her eyes flat and unemotional. *Can you help me with this?*

I deflated. *Sure.*

She explained her project again to me, even though I already knew about it. I got the feeling that she wanted to change the subject, and she seemed awfully tired. I sensed exhaustion in her signing, along with disinterest. She explained how she needed help with the English portion of her project, and I started to get a bit annoyed. *Just use the tree poem you already know!* I signed, aware that it came off as rather dismissive.

I don't know how! I could tell that she was just as annoyed as I was, and I took a deep breath. *Well. Haven't you read any books about trees or anything?*

She nodded. *Yeah, but not fiction. I don't think it can be a nonfiction book.*

I shrugged. All of a sudden, I too felt very tired. It was only Saturday morning, but between all the library excitement, homework had been pushed to the very last minute. It had been a stressful week, one of not nearly enough sleep. To top it all off, I stayed up late last night to finish reading my book. I didn't regret that part, but I still felt like I should've at least slept in a little later this morning to make up for it.

In the end, we both went over to the bookshelves, and picked out random books. Dad found us there a half hour later, after we had each been through two drinks, curled up on the coffee shop's couch, not talking, our noses buried in used books.

31. time

SINCE ROSEMARY HADN'T BEEN much help with my English assignment during our time at the coffee shop, I went home with no more progress than when I'd left. Benjamin greeted me at the door with a purr, and I again wondered why he had always preferred me to my sister. I figured that most people would rather be with her, so I guess it all balanced out.

I turned to go into my bedroom to think some more, when Dad grabbed my arm. *Not so fast,* he said. I raised my eyebrows in mock indignation.

Don't you think you should spend some more time out here with us? You're in your room all day.

I shrugged. *Don't Bother the Introvert, Dad. I*

signed with a smile, using the catchphrase my mom had coined years ago. My mom had loved people, and was very outgoing with people she knew well, but she was always hesitant among strangers. She always said it was her inner poet that liked being alone, but the rest of her loved human interaction. I liked this idea, that people could be two different things.

He nodded, sighed. *I barely see you girls anymore.*

I know. I have a lot of work to do. I had honestly thought I had not been spending as much time alone in my room as I used to. I often lost track of time, and was usually shocked when I glanced down at my wristwatch to see that hours had passed. Sometimes it felt like my time was spending me, rather than the other way around.

Dad nodded, letting me go. I went back into my room, but couldn't get anywhere with my project, so I ended up back in the living room, where Dad was watching a football game and Rosie was sprawled out on the floor with a book. It was a normal Saturday, and I grabbed a book off of one of the living room shelves and began to read on the couch. Benjamin curled up next to me, and I absentmindedly petted him while I read. I figured that cats were all natural introverts, and maybe that was why he often gravitated towards me. Rosemary's exuberance could be a bit much sometimes. But my sister didn't seem to mind. No one did, except for me.

As I thought, I looked at the little cat, realizing that he wasn't little anymore. We had gotten him at the beginning of the school year, which already felt like a very long time ago, but I was surprised to see how much Benjamin had grown. Time was a funny thing.

32. news (tRagically)

EARLY ONE MORNING in January, I awoke to the sound of the television downstairs. My clock told me it was only five-thirty. I crawled out of bed and crept downstairs, my curiosity overpowering my sleepiness.

What're you doing? I asked Dad, who was slouching in the recliner, looking as tired as I felt. *Watching the news,* he replied.

Now?

He shrugged. *You watch it now, and there's time for your day to get better.*

Oh. I sat down, but he was right, and there was no good news, and so I went back upstairs.

A couple days later, I happened to run into

Fern in the hallway when she was alone. "Can you meet me in the library at lunch tomorrow?" I asked. "There's news."

Her eyes lit up, and she nodded. "I'll be there." Fern seemed excited, although I hadn't told her whether it was good news or bad news. Sometimes, it seemed like tragically bad things only happened on TV, which I knew was not true. But I also knew that when something tragically bad happens to you, you spend a bit of time questioning whether or not it is real, as though it belongs on the television in your living room and not in your life.

That afternoon, we had orchestra practice. We had handed in our folders after the Christmas concert, but Fern and I had kept our notes, of course. We sat down as Mr. Alden talked about how proud he was of the progress we had made, and I knew that neither Fern nor I was really paying attention.

I thought about high school, and how I had expected something so vastly different from what I got. The first time I had walked through the halls of St. Michael's, I had convinced myself that I was going to a magical place in which I would do something magnificent.

In the mystery novels my mom used to read,

it seemed as though the detectives knew what they were doing, while I hadn't the faintest idea. Real-life high school was much more ordinary than I had expected. I found myself looking for mystery when none came my way. I still couldn't tell if this was a good thing.

I only snapped out of my reverie when Mr. Alden began passing out the new folders, the ones that would prepare us for the spring concert in a few months. Fern and I locked eyes across the room.

The folders looked the same, shabby black paper panels barely holding the packets of sheet music together. I peeled it open, shuffling through the music, barely registering the titles of the pieces. I flipped through the packet three times, finding nothing out of the ordinary. I glanced at Fern, who was shuffling through her music as well. She glanced at me after a moment, and I shook my head a little, feeling foolish, but also very detective-like.

I felt like maybe I was just living in a movie, and I was the protagonist, and the director always wanted me to be more dramatic, more theatrical, more. . .unnatural. For some reason I had a tendency to do these things, though a part of me always knew how strange some of them looked. I figured that this was just the result of my mother's love for poetry and theater, paired with my dad's methodical thinking. Audrey had evidently inherited more from Dad, along with some unaccounted traits that couldn't be traced to anyone in particular. Audrey was kind of the black sheep of the family, but in a way, we were a family of black sheep.

The next day, I met Fern in the library as promised. We were both there a little early. I beckoned her to the back, behind the shelves, which had become our little hideout. It felt secluded, even though we were, more often than not, the only ones in the library.

"So Audrey and I were at Ashton Coffee this weekend," I began, and proceeded to tell her in great detail all that I had heard. I was relieved that, unlike my sister, Fern seemed to share my enthusiasm. Perhaps she had expected something different from high school, too.

After I was finished, Fern blew out a big sigh. "Wow. This just keeps getting more and more complicated, doesn't it?"

I nodded. "But we're getting closer."

She looked hesitant. "Rosemary. . .do you really think we'll find anything? I mean, this could just be some disagreement between some random guy and his girlfriend. It could be a coincidence."

I nodded, a little surprised. "I guess, but aren't you hoping it's more than a coincidence?"

I could hear my mother's voice. *There are no coincidences.*

Fern shrugged. "I don't know. I don't want it to get to be much more than it already is, I guess. I don't want to get caught up in too much." She stopped, and tilted her head. I could almost see the gears turning inside her brain as she debated with herself. "But on the other hand, it could be nothing. I mean, won't you feel kind of silly if it turns out to be a different Miranda, and the notes are just a joke?"

I felt silly at that very moment, but I wasn't about to admit it. "Well, you don't have to stick around if you're not interested. Go back to your friends if you want. It's fine with me." It came out a bit harsher than I had expected, and I wasn't really sure why I was getting so worked up about this. "Sorry, I didn't mean-"

She cut me off. "No, it's fine. I want to keep looking, I really do, honest. Let's look through the yearbooks again."

"Really, if you don't want to-"

"No, I do." She stood up and walked over to the shelf that held the yearbook archives. She came back a moment later with an armful of yearbooks, and I stood up to grab the rest. We wordlessly searched through the books for a while with no success. It was oddly calming, I thought, just rifling through the yearbooks. After what felt like hours of searching, but in reality was only about thirty minutes, we finally found what we were looking for. It was one we had looked through before, having skimmed through the senior pages but nothing more.

I was thinking hard. Fern had gone back and forth on the issue so many times, and so had I, and we still didn't know if what we were doing was right. I was a little bit frustrated, mainly with myself, for not knowing how to handle myself and everything around me.

I was so deep in thought that I almost didn't see the name I was looking for on the page dedicated to the juniors. A picture caught my eye in the eighth row of students, and I snapped back from my thoughts. The name read "Miranda Perez."

And above the name was a picture of Miss Strayer.

33. hAlfway

I HAD NO IDEA why I was so caught up in this school project, but for a while I was sort of paralyzed in a half-finished state. That day I had given up was one of many, and I began to sink into a sort of desperation about it. I needed to finish, and not only for the substantial percentage of my grade it was covering.

A couple weeks later, Rosemary called a meeting at Ashton Coffee with Fern and me. I thought that she was taking this too far, but I also was beginning to get stressed out over the project, and didn't particularly want to leave the house if I didn't need to. But Rosemary seemed adamant, so I reluctantly agreed to go along with the plan.

Rosie and I arrived fifteen minutes early, and I swear it was the only time in her life Rosemary Lane Cooper was early to something. Fern arrived a little later, and we all gathered around the bookshelves, holding hot drinks and muffins. Fern surprised me by ordering unsweetened green tea. I had her pinned as a cappuccino girl, or something. One of those fancy drinks that fancy coffee shops only sold in styrofoam cups.

Rosie began the meeting in an exaggeratedly formal manner, swearing all to secrecy and glancing around to make sure the barista we presumed to be Miranda's boyfriend was not within earshot, even though we were not talking about him specifically.

Rosie looked like she was going to explode. Her signing burst out of her in big, sweeping gestures. *So Miss Strayer is Miranda! Mrs. Perez is Miranda's mom!*

We nodded. This fact had already been established.

So the barista is Miss Strayer's boyfriend.

Rosemary gasped as she said it, and I suppressed an eye roll at my sister's theatrics. I was not in the mood to play detective.

Once the meeting was under way, Fern and I

shared a look over our drinks. Rosie was taking this too seriously, we both knew. But we didn't want to let her down. I wanted to believe we were on a quest for justice, like she did, but I couldn't make myself believe it. And I was already too invested. I couldn't stop halfway.

So, Rosie was saying, *we have to reunite them. Somehow, they need to meet up.*

We nodded, more hesitantly this time. *Wait,* I said. *Wait. We're not supposed to know any of this, remember? If we do anything, they'll find out we were snooping around. And we could....mess things up.* They would find out that *Rosemary* was snooping around, I was thinking. But of course I couldn't say that.

She completely ignored my perfectly reasonable comment. *Wait! Wait a minute! What if everything that's been going on with Mrs. Perez is related to all this? What if she was crying because of something Miranda did?*

I shrugged, and Fern did the same. As the pieces came together, it was beginning to get difficult to be cynical about it. It all seemed to check out.

Fern said something, and Rosie absentmindedly translated for me. To a bystander, it might just have looked like she was fidgeting with something in her hands; her interpreting for me had become second-nature to her. I think sometimes she did it without thinking when I wasn't there. I watched her hands intently to catch Fern's message. *What if we ask the boyfriend? We can say we're friends of Miranda's and maybe he'd tell us something. If we're going to reunite them, then we need to know why they aren't talking in the first place.*

Rosemary stopped and considered this, but I shook my head. *No.*

My sister looked at me. *No?*

We can't do that.

She looked a little annoyed. *Why not?*

We can't just go up to him and ask what happened with Miranda and her mom. I mean, what if he tells Miss Strayer that we asked, and it gets back to her that we're trying to find out. That won't look good. And we could. . .make the problem bigger. The thoughts from the night of the concert were creeping back. *Every choice that we make. . .*

Rosie sighed. *We have to make sure they get reunited.* Her jaw was set hard, and her eyes were steady. At that moment, I could tell how much she felt that she needed to do this.

Fern sighed, deep in thought. She looked at us reluctantly, casually, with annoyance, but not directed at us. *I'll do it.* Rosie and I just looked at her.

Miss Strayer - Miranda - doesn't know me. If it gets back to her that we're looking, she won't know that you have anything to do with it.

It was a good point. Rosie agreed that this was the best course of action, but I didn't say anything.

Fern took a deep breath. *Okay. What should I say?*

Rosemary set her cup down on the coffee table in between us, pursed her lips. *Tell him that you're a friend of Miranda Strayer, and that - hmm. You could ask for her phone number maybe. Tell him you lost it. And when he tries to give it to you, ask some questions.*

Fern shook her head and chuckled. *Okay. Like what?*

You can ask him if he's her boyfriend, and maybe ask how her mom is doing?

Fern looked as unsure as I was feeling. *Okay. . . .what if he doesn't tell me?*

Rosie shrugged flippantly. *Then we leave. You'll probably never see him again anyway. Didn't you say the cafe across town has better tea, anyway?* Fern nodded and laughed. *Then we'll need a new hideout, I guess.*

I chimed in. *If he doesn't tell you, then say that you'll just ask Miranda. He is giving you her phone number, after all. If all goes well, that is.*

Fern started to laugh, nervously. *Why do I feel like I'm going on a mission into enemy territory?*

Rosie smiled, but her eyes were entirely serious. *Because you are.*

Suddenly something occurred to me. *Wait. Fern, you're what - fifteen? Is he going to think it's weird that you're friends with Miranda?* I knew it was not too big of a deal, but I had a very bad feeling about this, and felt the need to stop it.

Fern shrugged. *Then I'll improvise,* she said with a grin. I could tell she was beginning to have fun with it, and I became more uncomfortable.

Rosie smiled. *You could probably pass for sixteen or seventeen. Maybe even eighteen. You'll be fine. Or you could say your sister is her friend. Your sister's older, right?*

Fern nodded. *Okay, let's go.*

We watched her out of the corner of her eye as she bounced up to the checkout counter. She said something to the barista, and he pulled out a little pad of paper, not unlike the one I carried around. He began to write something on it, and she began talking again, tucking a strand of hair behind her ear. He replied, and she took the paper. They chatted a little longer, and she turned around with a little wave and strolled back to us.

Rosie had picked up a book to avoid watching Fern as she talked, but now she lowered the book a little, peeking over the top. Fern bounced back to us, glancing behind her. When she saw that the barista had gone in the back of the shop, and she waved the scrap of paper at us, a big, mischievous smile plastered on her face.

She sat back down in her chair, and took a sip of her tea. *The whiteboard says they have ice cream on Friday afternoons.*

Fern! I surprised myself by signing to her, but I was smiling. *What happened up there?*

My sister looked at me with a surprised expression, and then she smiled. *Yeah, Fern, what happened?*

Fern grinned. *I told him I was a friend of Miranda Strayer, and he seemed to believe me. My sister's had about a thousand boyfriends,* she added with a roll of her eyes, *so I know how to talk to them. So I said, "You're her boyfriend, right?" and he nodded. So good call, Rosemary.*

I said that I lost her phone number and just like

that, he went to give it to me. I said that I hadn't talked to her in awhile, and asked how her mom was doing.

He said that he didn't know. And he also said he didn't think Miranda knew, either. So maybe she knows her mom's alive, but doesn't want to talk to her.

Fern stopped talking, looked at us, and then looked away. *I didn't want to push my luck too much, but I asked one more thing.*

She looked a little unsure, as though she might have done something she shouldn't have. *I told him that I ran into Miranda's mom the other day, and she said hi. I said I'd pass it on, but I didn't have her phone number. So I. . .asked him to tell Miranda her mom said hi.*

Fern looked at us, barely meeting our eyes. *It occurred to me after we planned out the whole thing. I was already up there.*

Rosemary looked thoughtful, and I could see the wheels turning in her brain. *It was a good idea. One thing, though. If you had to "pass on the message," couldn't you just tell her yourself, since you got her phone number?*

Fern laughed. *You know, I was hoping he wouldn't pick up on that. Apparently he's not the brightest. Tell Miss Strayer she can do better than that,* she added with a chuckle.

Rosemary nodded, deep in thought. *Okay. So we know that he's her boyfriend, and that Miss Strayer - Miranda - knows her mom's alive, but doesn't want to talk to her. But why?*

I had been quiet this whole time. I was a bit unsure about this plan, but since the others were okay with it, and I couldn't think of anything better, I went along with it. I knew my sister would probably go ahead with her scheme whether or not I protested. I chimed in suddenly. *How do we know that this is something that should be fixed? If neither of them want to speak to the other, why should we - why would we - intervene?*

Rosie looked me in the eye. *Because it shouldn't be this way.*

I looked at Fern, who started talking again. *I think that if we can do something to make it better, we should.* I remembered what Rosemary told me about Fern's parents. *Plus, you said that Mrs. Perez was hanging around in Miss Strayer's neighborhood anyway, right? So, she wants to talk to her daughter. Unless that was just a coincidence.*

I tilted my head to one side. I hadn't put that together. If one of them wanted to reunite, was that enough to want to reunite them? I wasn't sure.

I tuned back into the conversation.

Rosemary was rapidly talking. I hoped they were keeping the volume down, since Barista was just around the corner. *So we could arrange a meeting. Maybe we could invite them both to some event, and make them sit together.*

Fern bunched her lips to the side. *Sounds like a lot of work.*

Rosie nodded. *Audrey, what do you think? I say we do it.*

I sighed. *Don't think it's a good idea. What if the meeting goes horribly and it's our fault?*

Then we try again. Or we don't. If it comes to that, we'll talk about it then.

I had a lot going on in my own life, and didn't particularly want to embark on this mission that my sister seemed so oddly passionate about. On the forefront of my mind was the school project, the due date of which was creeping closer and closer, while I was stuck in an inertial loop. Trying to reunite two people who didn't want to be reunited seemed pretty risky to me. Something else occurred to me just then. *Okay, what about this? Say the meeting goes well. Wouldn't we then have to explain why we know all this? Isn't this kind of stalker-ish?*

Rosie and Fern shrugged. My sister replied. *If it goes successfully, then they'll be thanking us. How we knew it won't really matter.*

Fern chimed in. *What about the notes, then? Are we assuming that Miranda wrote the poetry notes as well?*

Rosie nodded slowly. *I guess.*

So they weren't meant for us after all! Miranda graduated - what, eight years ago? Seven? Were they just left over from when she put them there?

Rosie's eyes were wide. *I don't know. Was Mrs. Perez teaching at St. Mike's back then? We should've checked the yearbooks for that, too.*

Fern nodded. *I think so. My sister graduated six years ago, and she had Mrs. Perez for Latin.*

I was beginning to zone out at this point, since the yearbook searching was something I hadn't been involved in in the first place, but this was the first I had heard of Fern's sister. *Did your sister know Miranda?*

Fern tilted her head, and I could tell by Rosemary's surprised expression that neither of them had thought of that. *We could ask her. She lives by herself now, so I don't see her a lot. We could go to the library after school and ask her. She works there.*

Rosie smiled at me. *I knew I kept you around for a reason,* she signed with a grin. I rolled my eyes playfully. *You know you only keep me around to help you with math.*

Fern glanced my way. *What time do you get out of school?*

Three fifteen. Why?

She did a quick calculation, looked at Rosemary. *We get out fifteen minutes earlier than she does. Can we walk and pick her up before we go to the library?*

Sounds great, Rosemary said.

Fern smiled. *Okay. Let's see. . .Jenna works every other day, so. . . does Tuesday work for you guys?*

Rosemary and I nodded in perfect unison. Fern giggled. *Your twin stuff can be a little alarming sometimes, you know that?*

I held out my fist to my sister, and she bumped it with hers. With our free hands we both signed the word "meow." We laughed; it was an inside joke that no one else knew.

After a while, we stood up and went our separate ways, with Fern going to great lengths to stay out of the barista's line of sight. The shop was close enough to Fern's house that she could walk home, but Rosie and I had to wait for Dad to come pick us up. We sat down on a metal park bench outside the shop, without talking. Rosie had bought yet another used book from the coffee shop, so she sat quietly, completely absorbed in what she was reading. As for me, I just watched the cars go by. It was strangely calming, just seeing the blurs of color zoom past, set against the backdrop of the mountains, faintly purple in the evening light. Eventually, one of the cars pulled into the lot, and Dad climbed out of the driver's seat. I had to tap my sister on the shoulder to snap her out of her literary world, and we clambered into the minivan to go home.

34. silence

THE NEXT FEW DAYS passed slowly, softly, silently. Audrey kept asking me for help with her project, and I began to look forward to the day when it would be finished.

When Tuesday finally arrived, Fern and I met in the courtyard after the last bell rang. Her black hair was pulled into a sleek ponytail, a simpler style than usual. I waved her over, and we began to walk. We chatted a little about orchestra, and about movies, and unimportant things. It was nice to talk about things that didn't matter. Or didn't seem to.

After the chatter had settled down, we walked in silence. It was the kind of silence that was comfortable, the kind in which you knew that both people just didn't feel like talking, and were okay with it. It was funny how Fern was one of the most talkative girls in school, always ready with a quip about a TV show, or about the latest hit single, or about something like that, but when she was with me and Audrey, she was much more genuine. She talked less, and when she did speak, her comments were much more thoughtful.

She spoke up after a while. "I keep thinking about what Audrey said. What if it doesn't go well and they blame us? I mean, this could be something big. We don't know enough to be - snooping around - like this."

I swallowed hard. I knew Audrey was right, but I think I didn't want it to be true with such an intensity that I had convinced myself otherwise. I didn't quite know how to articulate this, so I just nodded.

She went on. "Look, I know this means a lot to you, and I get it, but I'm not sure you're seeing the whole picture here. I know your family life has always been. . .I don't know. . .cozy and quiet and nice. . .but it's not like that for everyone. I mean, they could have good reason to want to get away from each other. Maybe Miranda's mom used to beat her, or made her leave, or - or something. Maybe it's better if they don't get back together."

I knew all this. I had known it for a while, but I didn't like how bluntly Fern was putting it. "I know. I know all that, but. . .we're so deep into this already. Do you really want to quit now, when we could really do something about it?"

"Rosemary, you're not a detective. You're a fourteen-year-old girl living in the suburbs. I want this to be a big movie mystery too, but it's not."

My voice was gradually rising. "This isn't about the adventure anymore. I know I can't go around trying to solve everyone's problems, Fern. I know that! I just. . .I can do something about this. And. . .I think I should."

She nodded, and sighed without meeting my eyes. "Sorry," she muttered softly, after a brief pause, her hands fidgeting awkwardly in her coat pockets.

I took a deep breath. "Yeah. Me too."

We were almost at Ashton Heights High School, and we spent the remainder of our walk in silence. This silence was different than before though. There were unsaid things hanging in the air between us.

Audrey was waiting for us in the front lawn

when we arrived. She waved, and came over to join us. At that moment, I was very glad to see her.

Twenty minutes later, we walked through the big doors of the library. It felt like we were walking into the place where we would find answers, and I hoped that that was the case. I was developing a sort of desperation as we got closer to the answer, or so I hoped. I had to finish what I started.

We found Fern's sister Jenna in the back of the library, behind a big, bulky computer. Her hair was green this time, pulled back in a ponytail not unlike Fern's, but paired with her dangling feather earrings and black eyeshadow, Jenna looked very different from her younger sister.

"Hey, Jenna," Fern said. Jenna looked up with black-lined eyes.

"Hey."

"These are my friends, Audrey and Rosemary," Fern continued. Jenna looked at me, then at Audrey, then back at me. Fern continued, an irritated edge to her voice. "Yes, they're twins." Audrey and I were not identical, but our hair was about the same length and light brown color. At first glance, a stranger might mistake one of us for the other, even though I am an inch taller and

Audrey's face is rounder.

"So, we wanted to ask you some questions," Fern said, leaning on her sister's cluttered desktop. "About when you went to St. Mike's."

"Um, okay. I have a break in ten minutes," Jenna said with a quick glance at a watch held to her wrist with a bundle of multicolored string. "Can we talk then?"

Fern nodded. "We'll look around a bit until then."

She beckoned us to the shelves. With a roll of her eyes she said, "Ten minutes until her break. Like she doesn't just sit there and do nothing all day." It occurred to me that maybe Fern didn't get along very well with her sister. I thought about what it would be like to have a sibling so much older than me. I did a quick calculation in my head. If Jenna graduated from high school six years ago, then she was nine years older than Fern, Audrey, and me. Having grown up with only one sibling who was just twenty-five minutes older than me, it was hard for me to imagine what that was like. The three of us chatted among the bookshelves while we waited for Jenna. It was quiet in the library, but not silent. The sound of shuffling pages and hushed whispers drifted through the shelves.

Jenna found us at a table near the window a few minutes later. We were sitting quietly, listening to the sounds of the library. She sat down across from Audrey, next to Fern, who stiffened, almost imperceptibly. "So, what do you guys wanna know?" Jenna asked.

Fern glanced at us. "Did you know Miranda Str- I mean, Miranda Perez?"

She nodded. "I think so. I knew who she was, at least. She was a year or two older than me, I think. Didn't graduate, if I remember correctly."

Fern nodded. "We'd heard that."

"Right, and she caused a big fuss about it, too. Nobody'd ever dropped out of St. Mike's before."

I spoke up. "So do you know why she dropped out?"

Jenna shook her hand in a *so-so* motion. "It's all rumors, really. I didn't really know Miranda, but word got around, you know? I heard she got in a big fight with her mom. A *really* big one."

"And her mom worked at the school, right?"

"Right. Mrs. Perez. Taught Latin, I think?"

We nodded. "So they fought about something, and she just - left? Ran away? What happened?"

Jenna shrugged, fiddled with her blue infinity scarf. "As far as I know, she left. During senior year, I think. I heard she lived with a friend until she got a place of her own. I always wondered how she did it."

I shook my head. Seventeen - even eighteen - seemed awfully young to be self-sufficient like that. "Do you know what the fight was about?"

Jenna shook her head, her green ponytail swishing. "Like I said, I didn't really know her. I heard quite a lot of rumors about it though, some of them pretty outrageous. I have no idea what really happened."

She tilted her head. "Why are you guys so interested in this?"

Fern, Audrey, and I glanced at each other. Fern shrugged. "We heard something about it in school. . . and we were curious."

Jenna narrowed her eyes at her sister. "Yeah? What did you hear?"

"Well. . ." Fern looked at me, trying to be inconspicuous, wondering what to say.

Jenna saw right through it. "Come on - what really happened?"

I looked at Fern, and she gave an infinitesimal nod. I took this as the okay to tell

Jenna what had happened.

"Long story short," I started, and even as I said it I knew that it would not be easy to make this story short. "Miss Strayer- I mean, Miranda Perez, or Miranda Strayer- anyway, the point is, it's the same person. She's my violin teacher. Fern and I have Mrs. Perez for Latin, and you see, we got these notes in our orchestra folders. We traced them back to an English textbook we found in the back of the library. We did some. . . digging around. . . and found out enough to put some of the story together. Miranda wrote them, and we know she didn't finish at St. Mike's, and we were. . . just wondering if you could tell us some more about it."

Jenna nodded slowly, thoughtfully. "Wow. So Miranda wrote these notes? And you just happened to find them?"

Fern and I shrugged. "I guess," I said.

"Do you think that happened by accident?"

I looked at Fern. Maybe it wasn't an accident. The possibility of that hadn't occurred to me. By the look on Fern's face, I concluded that she hadn't considered it, either. What if Miranda's notes hadn't ended up in our hands by accident? What if they were written for us? Could Mrs. Perez have put them there? I couldn't think of a reason for Miss

Strayer to be in the building once she left, but I supposed it was possible that she had put them there. For some reason, Jenna's words made me question all we had learned so far. "Accident" was such a large mysterious concept that seemed far too unlikely.

I brought my thoughts back to the present, and I thought for a moment about all that I knew about Miss Strayer. She played far too many instruments, she had a slight hoarding problem, she liked colorful things and coffee. I knew that she had had a fight with her mother, and didn't speak with her anymore. I knew that she dropped out of high school and that she was dating a barista who worked at Ashton Coffee. What else did I know about her? I racked my brain. I remembered something that she had told me on my first day of violin lessons.

"She went to college!" I blurted out. "She said she has a twin brother, and that they didn't get along. But she missed him when they went to college."

Fern nodded slowly. "Huh," she said. "So, she dropped out of high school and went on to college. Can you do that?"

"I guess so? Jenna, did Miranda's brother go

to St. Mike's?" It seemed unlikely, as we would probably have noticed another Perez in the yearbook.

The older girl shrugged. "I didn't even know she had a brother. Listen, I have to go back to work soon. There's really not much else I could tell you, anyway." She gave us a little wave as she stood up. "Nice meeting you two," she said to me and Audrey.

"You too," I said, and Audrey smiled.

We watched Jenna leave, and then despite all my worries, I surprised myself by laughing. It felt a bit like the relief I had experienced after the winter concert, when Dad and Audrey and I sat on the couch and talked. It was as though all my nervousness had bubbled up inside me all of a sudden and exploded forth in a burst of laughter. "What on earth did we get ourselves into?" I wondered aloud.

Fern slowly shook her head. "I know," she said, "it's getting to be more than we bargained for."

I became a little unsure, considering the conversations I'd had with both of them. I knew that neither Fern nor Audrey was as enthusiastic about this as I was.

"You guys okay with this?"

Fern nodded. "I'm in."

"Audrey?"

I had been signing the conversation to her, but she hadn't really been contributing to the discussion. I looked over at her. She seemed deep in thought, and I hoped that she had been paying attention. My sister could sometimes zone out so far that she couldn't even register a conversation happening around her. But now, she looked me in the eye. *I think we should help.* But her eyes were nervous.

I smiled faintly. "Are you sure? What changed your minds?"

Fern shrugged, her expression guarded. "Just learning more about it, I guess," she said, not meeting my eyes. I wondered if her real reason had something to do with her own parents, or her sister.

I looked at Audrey, who fidgeted wordlessly with her hands for a moment, which was more my habit than hers. *Even if they don't want to talk to each other. . .*she trailed off, lapsing back into fidgeting with her fingers, with the hem of her sweatshirt. *They should,* she finished.

We had settled into another silence, this one heavy, especially in contrast to the lighthearted laughter of just a few moments ago. It was a deep silence, one that filled the ocean between us with unsaid words.

35. labels

THE FIRST THING I NOTICED when I met Fern Reynolds was the labels that were plastered all over her clothes. I had noticed the same thing at my school; kids went around like walking advertisements for their favorite stores. None of them wore as many brand names as Fern, though.

Labels are a funny thing. You can label shirts, or school assignments, or people. The thing about labels is that they change the way you look at something. Maybe some people see Fern differently when she wears a Forever 21 shirt than when she doesn't, but I've never seen her any differently. People will look at a homework assignment differently when they see that it's labeled as a quiz.

And people look at me differently when they find out that I'm deaf. Or when they find out that I read physics papers for fun but can't sustain a conversation. It's as though they're mentally putting a label on the front of my shirt, but this time it's not for a store.

Needless to say, I hate labels.

In Fern's defense, none of her labels advertised outrageously expensive stores. I knew that she wasn't trying to flaunt her wealth. But something in the back of my mind told me to be wary of her. I thought that just maybe, the kind of person who wore those kinds of labels was the kind of person who would put labels on people, too.

Fern had been nothing but nice to me so far, but something still held me back from becoming as close with her as Rosemary was. Maybe I was intimidated, or just confused. I was continuing to participate in this "mystery" for Rosemary's sake as much as mine. I knew that she felt bad for me, and I didn't want pity. So I figured, maybe Dad was right, and I should try to get out a little more. Although, this was very far from what I had had in mind when he had said that.

The Saturday after our meeting with Jenna, I sat at the dining room table with my least favorite textbook splayed out in front of me like a butterfly pinned down on a corkboard. There were thousands of poems in my English textbook, none of which I could even begin to understand. After a half hour of reading words that might as well have been in a different language, I lay my head down on the table with a sigh. Why did I have to do an English project, anyway? I sure as heck wasn't going to be a poet.

I suddenly thought about my conversation with Rosemary, the one in which we'd talked about Mom. I never liked poetry, but my mom didn't mind. That was one of my favorite things about her. She was so passionate about the things she loved, but she never minded if someone didn't share her enthusiasm. She let us have our own enthusiasm.

I took a deep breath and pulled my head up. What had Rosemary said? That poetry was just laying out the process of figuring out what to say. I opened up to a random page in my textbook, and found a short Emily Dickinson poem. My mom's favorite poet. The one that had gotten her killed.

"The Brain is Wider Than the Sky" the title read. What did that mean?

I read the second line. "For put them side by side,"

And the third, "And one the other will contain,"

I tried to look at it as a progression of thoughts, and it began to make sense. Although the sky is literally much bigger than the brain, we can fit more in our minds than in the sky, so in a way, the brain *is* wider than the sky. It was just a long, rambling, lovely chain of thoughts.

I thought about Dad saying I spent too much time in my head. Maybe he needed to read this poem. How can a person not spend too much time in her head when inside her head is an entire universe? How can you *not* get lost in it? I read a few more Dickinson poems. It was poetry, but in a simpler form. One that made sense to me.

A few days later, I was still thinking about the poems. On a whim, I went into the basement, walking over to one of the big wall-to-wall bookshelves full of novels and poetry and other genres I don't enjoy reading. I pulled out a scrapbook of my mom's poems, and began to read. I hadn't read any of them in years, if ever.

I read one in particular, titled *The Modern Girl,* and paused. I read it again. It described exactly that: the modern girl. The girl with nice clothes and a lot of friends and an impossibly busy schedule.

She was much more than that, but it was sometimes difficult to see. It highlighted the beauty in conformity, which was strange, because I had always thought of my mother as a bit of a nonconformist. The funny thing was that it sounded just like Fern.

Perhaps I did some labeling of my own.

36. plans

ONE NIGHT, NOT LONG after our meeting with Jenna in the library, I couldn't sleep. When I was really little, I had a lot of sleepless nights. I was never worried or overly hyper; I simply would not fall asleep. It wasn't frequent enough for an insomnia diagnosis or anything, but even if it was, I don't think that my parents would have had me checked out for it anyway. When it became clear that Audrey did things her own way, in her own time, my parents refused to take her to a psychologist. My mother didn't believe in labels. She always said that if it had gotten bad, they would have taken her to see someone, but it never got to that point. Yes, she was different, my mother had said, but she was doing fine in her own way, and isn't that the best anyone can do?

My parents never told me any of this. As far as they were concerned, I recognized that my sister and I were different, but nothing beyond that. The only reason I know the rest is because of all those nights that I couldn't sleep. My bed used to be right up against an air conditioning vent, and I could sometimes catch fragments of conversation floating up the vent. Whenever I couldn't sleep when I was really little, Mom would come upstairs and we would chat for a little while until I felt like I could sleep. Those were the few times I could be with her alone.

I have always been pretty fidgety, and it was just hard for my body to calm down. I think that that is part of the reason that I love music so much. Playing an instrument gives purpose to my fidgeting fingers.

Anyway, when I couldn't fall asleep, I would talk with my mother. This was my first night in a while that I was having some trouble, so naturally I was thinking of her. I pulled out a binder from under my bed, where I had compiled some of her miscellaneous poems after she died. None of them had ever been published; they were the ones she wrote for fun, when she wasn't working. They had always been my favorites. I read through a few, smiling. They were about anything and everything, but all of them were hers, and I loved them.

Suddenly I remembered all the conversations I'd had with Audrey about Mom, like when you wake up really fast and all your memories come at you in a flash. We had talked about Mrs. Perez and Miss Strayer as though it was a situation we could not understand in our own lives. It was not true. We understood it, or thought we did. I hadn't really allowed myself to think about it that way.

Now, with nothing but silence and darkness drifting in from the air conditioning vent, I allowed the thoughts to creep in. If I found out that my mother was still alive, there was nothing she could have possibly done that would keep me from seeing her, no matter how angry I was. I closed my eyes.

Something Audrey had told me once popped into my head. Something about trees. She said that old trees who could communicate the farthest were called "mother trees." It was interesting, I thought, how they were called mother and not father. All throughout history, men have dominated the world, but the wisest of the trees were still called "mother." The name seemed to fit.

I rolled the idea around in my mind like a grape in my mouth. If Mommy was still here, would we still be homeschooled? Would I have met Fern? Would I have met Miss Strayer, or Mrs. Perez? Thoughts swirled like leaves in the wind, leaves blown from the mother tree to places far, far away.

Miranda, I thought, don't let this go to waste.

I hoped that we could do something. I hoped with all I had that I could save someone else's relationship with their mother from breaking off like mine had.

I smiled, and realized that I had been crying. It had been four years; I wondered if I would ever stop crying about it. I was done crying for the day, though. I climbed out of bed, grabbed a notepad and a pencil, and climbed back under the covers. I propped myself up on a pile of pillows, and began to plan.

"How to," I began, and then realized that I wasn't sure what I was trying to do in the first place. How to fix a family? How to help a hurting mom? How to calm an angry daughter?

I left it at "How To," and started on the

important part. How was I going to accomplish this? I jotted a few things down, crossed them out, rewrote them. I could invite them both to a party, or another event. There were several flaws in that one. For one, I knew neither of them well enough to invite them to a party. Two, I had never thrown a party in my life and didn't know the first thing about it. Third, a plan that elaborate would have to involve Dad, and while I knew that what I was doing was the right thing, I had my doubts as to whether he would agree. And so I had decided to keep the majority of the conundrum to myself. That is, between Audrey and Fern and Jenna and me.

Another idea was that I could invite Miss Strayer to a school event that I knew Mrs. Perez would be present at. While this option was slightly more viable than the last, it would still require some careful planning. The spring concert was rapidly approaching. I could invite Miss Strayer to see how my violin playing had progressed. I turned the idea over, searching for flaws. While Miss Strayer could certainly refuse the offer, if she accepted, the plan would then be fairly simple.

I was finally beginning to get tired, and I looked up to the ceiling, silently thanking Mom.

I set the pad of paper down on the floor

beside my bed, and looked around the room for Benjamin. As usual, he was nowhere to be found, probably sleeping in Audrey's room, as he often did. But I didn't care. I had a plan.

37. power (waVelength)

SOMETIMES I THINK about sound. I know about sound waves, and wavelengths, and how it's supposed to work. I also know about what went wrong inside my own head that prevented me from ever experiencing it. I don't mind, though. I'm not jealous of the hearing.

But, I still wonder what it's like. I once read that it's nearly impossible to explain to a blind person what sight is, and I think it's the same with the deaf. Sound waves and frequencies can't explain what my sister feels when she plays her violin.

The week before my project was due, I decided to analyze "The Sound of Trees" by Robert Frost. I'm not sure what brought me to my decision, but I realized eventually that while it was not the perfect choice, there was no perfect choice. I wrote an analysis of poetic form, that is, laying out the process of my thinking on the page. I discussed how trees do not speak in language as we understand it, that while they do not emit sound waves or codify messages, they communicate in other ways. I explained how their network of communication is not visible, or audible, or in any way tangible. This was my favorite part; their communication is not conventional, or normal in the way we understand it, but it is the less conventional methods that stay around the longest. Trees have probably been doing this longer than humans have walked the earth, and yet we didn't even know it until the twentieth century.

I finished my project less than a week before the deadline, the latest that I had ever finished any major school assignment. Later that day, Rosemary and I went back to the library with Fern, for another "meeting." Jenna wasn't working that day, so it was just the three of us. Rosemary had wanted to meet at Ashton Coffee again, but Fern had objected, concerned about whether the barista would recognize her. If he had talked to Miranda, then he may have had some inkling of the ruse, and we wanted to retain our anonymity, at least for now. Rosie's excited ramblings about it had begun to sound like she was starting up a secret organization. This made me slightly nervous, but I supposed it could be fun.

Since the library was too far from home to walk, Dad had dropped us off a few blocks from the library. It was a nice day, one of those days when you start to believe that spring just might come after all, so we had decided to go for a little walk around town before we met Fern at the library.

The trees were bare, but the soft breeze said that spring was just around the corner. The New England winters were harsh, but the springs were beautiful. We were in the in-between days, where it was technically spring, but still looked like winter. It felt like neither, like the transition between spring and winter was a season of its own. I liked the in-between times; the days could be anything you liked.

We strolled up and down Main Street for a while, just looking in the stores, watching people watching people watching people.

After a while, we went into the library doors, and found Fern already sitting there. We walked over to her table, and sat down. She surprised me by signing, clumsily but clearly. *Hey guys, how are you?*

My eyes widened. Smiling, I replied. *Pretty good. You?*

She laughed, and shook her head, saying something out loud to Rosemary, who translated. *Sorry. I'm just learning. Don't know too much yet.*

I grinned. *No problem. That's so cool that you're even learning it.*

She nodded, shrugged, smiled at me. *So what's this meeting about, Rosemary?* We both turned to my sister. I had been wondering the same thing. Rosie took a deep breath.

I've been thinking, she started, and I remembered that those words were the very same words that Dad had used to tell us about going to school. *I've been thinking. . .you girls are so smart,* he had started. Rosemary continued. *The spring concert is coming up. . .*she trailed off, then continued, in brief phrases interspersed with pauses. *Mrs. Perez will be there. And. . .if I invite Miss Strayer. . .*

Fern and I glanced at one another as we realized what she meant. *You can reunite them,* Fern finished for her.

Rosemary nodded. *There will be a ton of people there, but we could make it happen. And it won't look like we forced it.*

This was true. I realized, then, just how much power we had. I wasn't sure if I liked it. I realized that Rosemary had chosen not to tell me this before our meeting with Fern. Maybe she didn't want to explain it twice, or she wanted Fern there when I found out. I didn't like having that kind of power, either.

I looked at my sister. *How do you know that she'll agree to come?*

Rosie shrugged. *I don't. But I think she will.*

Fern raised her eyebrows and nodded. *I guess that's good enough. Works for me.*

I nodded too, taking a deep breath. *Sure. Let's do it.*

I smiled, but my mind was telling me otherwise. *This is wrong this is wrong this is wrong,* it said, with frustrating persistence. On the other hand, it could be right, I thought back. It was kind of like my failed experiment. If we left things where they were, Miss Strayer and Mrs. Perez would become the cat in the closed box. In other words, we would have started something, left it behind, and abandoned them in an in-between state, like the cat that was both alive and dead.

I hadn't thought about it that way before,

but I forced myself to tune back into the conversation Fern and Rosemary were having.

Can't believe the concert's only a week away, Fern was saying.

Rosemary nodded emphatically. *I know, right? It feels like the winter one happened just yesterday!*

Fern nodded solemnly. *But so much has happened since then.*

I nodded, and Rosemary glanced my way. I had never explained what had happened that night, after all. She looked away when she saw my expression. I had tried my best to block it out, but the memories kept seeping through the cracks, and my sister could tell.

I tried to change the subject. *So, what songs are you playing in the concert?* I asked.

They told me, and I tried to stay present in the conversation. There were a lot more people in the library this time than there had been when we had talked to Jenna, and the constant stream of people coming in and out the doors was distracting. Several times, I caught myself zoned out, just watching. There were all sorts of people wandering the sidewalks, but only a few filtered into the library.

I kept catching fragments of Fern and Rosemary's conversation, and then tuning back out. *And then I thought to myself, why on earth was I doing this?* Fern said at some point after they had diverged from the topic of the concert and had moved on to something else that I was not following.

I thought to myself. . .was there any other way to think? Can you think to someone other than yourself?

Maybe it was just one of those tricks that made the English language unnecessarily complicated, but maybe it wasn't. Maybe there are different types of thinking. I know that there's a surface level of thinking, the things that you are actively thinking about, like when I thought about experiments or worked through a complex math problem. But there are other levels to it, too, like when I thought about Mrs. Perez, but really I was thinking about my mom.

It was like a skyscraper. If you look at a skyscraper from above, you will only see what's happening on the roof, but you know that something is happening on all the floors of the building. I guessed that each floor is a level of thinking, and the closer you get to the ground, the farther away the thoughts are. But on every level of the building, a different thought happens, independent from all the others. As the stories of the skyscraper get closer to the ground, you have less and less power over the thoughts. Perhaps on the lower levels, there were thoughts that weren't even directed at *you*, per se. Maybe they were just there.

38. soldiErs

MY HEART WAS BEATING FAST as I dialed Miss Strayer's phone number. *Is deception okay if it has a higher cause?* I had asked Audrey earlier. She looked at me with a confused expression. *How high is the cause?* I shrugged and she eventually replied with a noncommittal *I have no idea.*

The phone rang several times, and I began to hope that maybe I would just have to leave a message. But on the fifth ring, I heard her pick up the receiver.

"Hello?" came Miss Strayer's voice tinnily from the other end.

"Hi, Miss Strayer," I began. "It's Rosemary Cooper."

"Hey, Rosemary! How are you doing?"

"I'm good. . ." I took a breath, but she started talking before I got a chance to continue.

"That's good to hear! How's your violin coming along?"

"Actually, that's what I wanted to talk to you about." I said, as naturally as I could. "My spring concert for orchestra is this Saturday. I was wondering if you might want to come watch."

She paused. "That's wonderful! I'd absolutely love to come, Rosemary, but my schedule is a little up in the air right now. Can I get back to you in a few days?"

I nodded, and abruptly realized that she couldn't see me. I wasn't used to talking on the phone. "Sure!"

"Ok, that's great. Thanks so much for inviting me, Rosemary. That means a lot."

If only she knew, I thought. We said goodbye and I hung up, with what was quite possibly too much enthusiasm. When one movie character tells another movie character to "act natural," I had never before realized how difficult that could be. Or maybe it was just the state of my acting skills, which were practically nonexistent.

A few days later, I received a phone call. I

hastily scooped up the receiver. "Hello?"

Miss Strayer's voice came back at me. "Hi! Is this Rosemary?"

"Yep!"

"I would love to come to your concert. This Saturday, right?"

I smiled. "Yep, this Saturday. So you're coming?"

"I'll be there!"

I said goodbye, hung up, and raced into Audrey's room to share the news.

That Saturday came quickly, and as I got ready for the performance, I thought about our plan, and what would happen if it went successfully. I'd feel better, of course, but would anyone else? What if it really was the wrong thing to do? I squashed these doubts down into the back of my mind, and focused on brushing my tangled hair.

Half an hour later, we piled into the minivan, which was beginning to make some odd noises. With a concerned look on his face, Dad hesitantly turned on the ignition. The car started, but didn't sound happy about it. We set off, hoping it would make it to our destination.

Within five minutes of the ten-minute drive,

the car began to sputter. "Come on, come on," Dad was muttering under his breath. I glanced in the backseat, where Audrey sat in a simple yellow dress. We shared a look, both an expression of exasperation and a shared smile at Dad's insistent talking to the car. The minivan had served us for twelve years, during which Dad had found it to be a suitable, if quiet, companion. My dad had an odd obsession with cars. It was odd because he loved our old battered minivan as much as he admired the Corvettes that we only ever saw on television. While I knew he would be disappointed if it had to go, that was not the primary concern at the moment. I glanced at my wrist, where I was wearing my mom's old watch, a simple clock with a thin silver band. The concert started in an hour, but I was supposed to be there in ten minutes.

Suddenly, the sputtering noises became more insistent, harder to ignore, and a couple lights on the dashboard began to blink. Dad sighed, exasperated. He pulled over, and stared at his hands on the steering wheel for a while before stepping out of the car. We watched him as he opened the hood of the car and fiddled with the engine. After a couple minutes of this, during which Audrey and I sat silently and watched, he got back in the driver's seat. Staring straight ahead, he opened his mouth to say something, and then closed it. Eventually he said, "I feel like an awful parent, but it's not too far to walk, right?"

I shook my head. "Walking always wakes me up a little. It'll be good before I perform."

He shook his head in exasperation. "Of course, it would give out today. Today of all days."

I was in too good of a mood to let this discourage me or my troops. "It's okay," I said. "I'll get there in time to practice, and you and Audrey can catch up."

He nodded grimly. "How about you and Audrey go together? In case. . . in case I can't get there in time, she'll get to see it." He paused, and looked at me. "I'm sorry, Rosie."

I nodded. "Dad, it's okay. Really." I clambered out of the passenger seat. I grabbed my violin and water bottle, and looked down the street. We were only a few blocks from the school, but still I hoped we would get there in time. *Come on, Audrey.*

She got out of the car and stood next to me. We waved to Dad, who was already on the phone with a car towing service, and we were off. We walked down the sidewalk, and I marveled at how strange we must look to passersby - me with my black gown and fancy hair, Audrey dressed up like she was going to a party. I bounced down the sidewalk, strangely excited but also vaguely distant.

We walked with purpose, looking only ahead, like soldiers going into battle. We didn't say a word as we walked along the street, the little shops that we had grown up in looking small and insignificant among the giant skeletons of trees towering above them. I knew that the trees would soon be in bloom, but it was striking how dead they looked. With some things, I knew, you just had to wait and see.

After a few minutes, with too little time to spare, we walked up the steps to the St. Michael's Preparatory School Auditorium. Audrey hadn't seen my last performance, and I wondered what she was thinking. I hoped she was looking forward to it. I was curious to see how she reacted to the auditorium when it was full and brimming with music. I told her to just find a seat and wait for Dad, and I went up to the stage, slipping behind the heavy curtain. Most of the kids were already there, and I gave a little wave as I sat down in my assigned seat, next to Fern's empty chair. I was glad to discover that I was not the last one to arrive.

We had had our last few rehearsals in the auditorium, to prepare for the big day, but it looked different today, for some reason. I looked around, trying to place the discrepancy. A hushed whisper drifted among the kids, as they nervously chatted to one another. The holiday decorations were still stacked at the back of the stage, already waiting for next Christmas. The lights were dimmed, and it gave the room an eerie glow.

I was sitting near the middle of the group, in the front row, and if I moved a little to the side, I could just get a peek out of the gap in the curtain. There were only a few visitors in the audience now, and it didn't take me long to find my sister. Audrey sat near the front, which surprised me, looking around as people filtered into the theater, meandering around a bit before settling on a particular seat.

"Hey, Rosemary," I heard. I whipped my head around, and saw Fern walking over to me, her violin tucked under her arm, a smile on her face.

"Hi, Fern," I replied. "You ready?"

"For which part?" she asked, sitting down next to me, tucking her violin beneath her chair. "The concert or the big reunion?"

I shrugged. "Both, I guess."

She shrugged back. "I have no idea. We'll just have to see."

I nodded. That seemed to be the case with most things. I nervously peeked out of the gap in the curtain again, hoping that Dad would get here in time. I wondered if he had gotten the car towed yet, and how he planned to get here. I couldn't see him in the audience yet, but as I looked, I spotted a familiar face sitting next to Audrey. Miss Strayer. She was here.

I watched as Audrey dug out her pad of paper and a pen, so they could chat for a little while. I marveled at how talkative my sister had become lately. In the beginning of the year, she had become more and more reclusive, but these days, she was only coming further and further out of her cave. I watched as Miss Strayer tapped Audrey's shoulder, taking her attention away from the paper she was furiously scribbling on. I couldn't make out what Miss Strayer signed to her, but I could see the huge grin spread across Audrey's face, and I realized I was grinning, too.

Fern looked over at me. "What is it?" she asked.

I pointed out to the crowd, scooting over in my chair so Fern could see out of the little gap between the curtains. "Wow," she said. "That's awesome."

I nodded. "It sure is."

We both watched for a little longer as Audrey and Miss Strayer conversed. "So this is really happening," I finally said.

She nodded slowly. "I guess so. I'm a little nervous."

"Me, too."

We lapsed back into silence as we watched the remainder of the musicians come backstage. Mr. Alden, looking very dapper in a pressed suit with his conducting baton, began to organize us, giving us his signature pre-concert pep talk that did little to motivate us, but always served to make us laugh, which I guess was just as effective.

After a while, the house lights began to dim, and we fidgeted in our seats, some of us nervous, some of us excited, some of us hungry for the glare of the spotlight in our eyes. Fern and I took a deep breath and shared a meaningful look as Mr. Alden slipped between the curtains to introduce us. We heard his voice blaring in the speakers, and I watched Dad hurry in, just as the curtain rose, looking frazzled and disheveled as he scanned the audience for Audrey. After a moment, he found her and Miss Strayer near the front, and managed to sit down just as the curtain reached the top of the stage.

I took a deep breath as the spotlights began to shine in my eyes, blotting out my view of the audience. My least favorite thing about performing in an orchestra was the fact that I couldn't see my audience in the glare of the floodlights, but even so, it was a glorious feeling when the curtain rose. It felt like an adrenaline rush even though I was not nervous about performing.

Mr Alden gestured for us to get into position, and I tucked my violin under my chin, holding the bow suspended above the strings.

At the first dip of his baton, I drew the bow across the first string, savoring the hum of the orchestra just beginning to open up. I swayed a little with the music as it swelled and fell, picturing Audrey's wide eyes taking it all in. My eyes glanced up from my music every once in a while to watch Mr. Alden, taking in the wild dance that was conducting. It was fabulous to watch, even without the added experience of the music.

All too soon, the piece was over, and I sighed contentedly. There was something euphoric about performing with other people, something wonderful about being a small part of something so much bigger than you - a symphony conducted by somebody else.

39. rings

THE EXPERENCE OF BEING at Rosemary's concert was like nothing I had ever experienced before. I could feel the music as it swelled and fell, like the ocean waves carrying me away. I could feel the piece as a whole, but I could also feel the independent movement of each instrument. There were layers and layers and layers to it, organized to fit perfectly together, like a Russian matryoshka doll. Each part fit perfectly inside the others.

I suddenly thought about tree rings. I had read an article about them when researching my project, and for some reason, I really liked the idea. Most people know that they can tell you how old the tree is, but they can tell you much, much more.

They can tell the weather throughout the tree's life, and when there was a drought, or a year of a lot of rainfall, or a year when the tree grew a lot, or a little. I loved this because it shows the layers to everything. Even something as ordinary as a tree has layers of beauty, layers of things inside of it, just like the orchestra. Everything was far more complex than we realized, and it was lovely.

In the beautiful organized chaos of the concert, I didn't realize that Dad had sat down next to me until the break between the first and second piece. I looked over and smiled, wondering how long he'd been sitting there.

All through the second piece, I closed my eyes, just feeling.

The concert was over much too quickly. The lights came on in the house far sooner than I would have expected or would have liked. I blinked fast in the sudden brightness. I glanced over at Miss Strayer, suddenly aware of her eyes watching me behind her round glasses. At my perplexed look, she began to sign something, then simply held out her hand for the pad of paper we had been using for conversation that was more advanced than her signing so far.

You really loved that, didn't you?

Confused, I nodded.

She turned back to the paper. *I could tell.* She was smiling. *Audrey, have you ever considered playing an instrument?*

I tilted my head to the side, and then shook it. *No.*

She nodded. *Think about it for me, okay?*

I was confused. *Can deaf people play instruments?*

She nodded. *Do you know about Beethoven?* she wrote. *Beethoven was deaf, and he wrote nine symphonies.*

I looked back at the stage, where the curtain had gone down. I turned the idea over and over in my mind, thinking hard. *I'll think about it,* I told her.

She smiled. *Good.*

All of a sudden, I noticed Mrs. Perez, sitting on the side of the theater, by the side door with a group of teachers. I remembered what was about to happen, and the euphoria of the concert slowly dissipated. The sinking feeling I had experienced before was beginning to return.

I could pinpoint the exact moment that Miss Strayer noticed her mom. She scanned the theater with her eyes, and her gaze lingered on Mrs. Perez for just a second too long. Her eyes widened, almost imperceptibly, and she rapidly turned away. I wouldn't have noticed her hesitation unless I had been looking for it. I continued to watch Miss Strayer out of the corner of my eye. She glanced down at her hand, where a ring I hadn't noticed before hung on her ring finger. Was she engaged? Married? It hadn't occurred to me that her last name was different from her mother's, and I wondered why that was. I realized suddenly how very little I knew about her, despite all of our searching. Maybe her parents were separated, or maybe Strayer was a family name she had taken on. The "Miss" that preceded her name indicated that she was not married, but I wondered anyway. Everything was more complex than we realized.

Miss Strayer and Dad talked for a while, and eventually Rosemary came out from backstage. There was a small reception in the lobby of the auditorium, with coffee and snacks. Dad and Miss Strayer showered Rosemary with compliments and praise of her playing, and we began to make our way back to the lobby. I walked behind Dad and Miss Strayer with Rosemary and Fern, who chatted about the performance for a while. As we reached the lobby, I noticed Mrs. Perez immediately, sitting at a table towards the middle of the cavernous room. I could tell that Rosie and Fern noticed her too, and we collectively glanced towards Miss Strayer, who was chatting with Dad. Apparently, she hadn't noticed yet.

She knows she's here, I signed to Fern and my sister. Rosemary nodded, whispering my message to Fern.

So, how are we going to do this? Rosemary asked. *They shouldn't talk in front of everybody.*

Fern nodded. *We need to get them alone somehow. Or at least with just us.*

We have to make sure that Mrs. Perez doesn't leave early. We'll have to keep an eye on her.

We picked a table, gravitating towards the edge of the room. I sat down between Rosemary and Fern, across from Miss Strayer, Dad, and Jenna. Fern's parents weren't there.

The adults were talking pretty intently, so we felt safe enough to discuss our plans, with Rosemary translating my messages to Fern in a hushed whisper. I realized that I had to make sure Miss Strayer couldn't see our signing.

Every once in a while, Jenna would contribute to the conversation. Fern hadn't filled her sister in about our latest plans, so we explained the main points to her while Miss Strayer was in the bathroom.

We were trying to be inconspicuous, but we were failing, and we knew it.

When Miss Strayer returned, we turned our conversation to more trivial things, like the concert, and movies, and Miss Strayer's hair, which was in thin, twisted braids, dotted with colored beads and swept up on top of her head. She looked quite elegant.

Over donuts and coffee we laughed, and watched as a light snowfall began outside. The high-ceilinged room was full of people eating and talking and laughing. Usually these situations made me a bit uncomfortable, but it was strangely soothing, just watching a bunch of very different conversations unfold among a bunch of very different people.

Suddenly a shadow fell over our table, and I looked up. A big woman stood over our table, her hair styled in a familiar braided updo. It was Mrs. Perez.

Rosemary and I locked eyes as we both turned to look at her. Mrs. Perez said something, and Rosie quickly interpreted for me. *You did marvelous, Rosemary. And Fern, your playing was amazing.* My sister and Fern smiled nervously, the same expression that Mrs. Perez was wearing. *Thanks, Mrs. Perez,* Rosemary said. Out of the corner of my eye, I could see Miss Strayer's head snap upwards to look. Her eyes widened, just as imperceptibly as they had when she first noticed her mother's presence in the auditorium during the concert. Mrs. Perez turned her gaze to Dad. *Mr. Cooper. How nice to see you again. Your daughter did a wonderful job.* He nodded, apparently completely oblivious to the tangible sense of tension.

Dad, out of his extreme, ever-present, fabulously ill-timed politeness, began to go around the table. *This is Rosemary's violin teacher, Miss Strayer.*

Miss Strayer's eyes widened. *We've met.* She said it curtly and dismissively.

Dad nodded, looking vaguely puzzled.

Mrs. Perez opened her mouth to say something, and promptly closed it again. She seemed at an utter loss for words. Miss Strayer, as though nothing had happened, turned back to Jenna, continuing their previous conversation.

Miranda. Mrs. Perez looked at her daughter with pleading eyes. *Can we talk?*

Miss Strayer looked at her mother indignantly. *Not now.*

Mrs. Perez swallowed hard, and sat down at the empty seat beside Fern. Even Dad finally recognized the obvious discomfort of the situation.

Miss Strayer stared. *What are you doing?* She looked more angry than I had ever seen her. In fact, I wasn't sure if I had ever seen her angry.

Mrs. Perez just looked at her, matching her gaze, trying to communicate with only her eyes.

Can we please do this later? Miss Strayer tried to calm her voice as she gestured to the rest of us, who were collectively unsure about what was going on. She took a deep breath. *Please.* Rosemary was signing underneath the table, so that Miss Strayer wouldn't know that she was passing on the information to me.

Mrs. Perez wordlessly stood up, apparently trying to suppress tears. She began to walk away, and then looked back with a glance at our table. *I'm sorry.*

Miss Strayer stared at the table for a moment, before echoing what her mother had said just a moment before. *I'm sorry.* She stood up, and followed Mrs. Perez, who was headed for the door. We inconspicuously watched as she grabbed her mother's arm to stop her. They talked for a little while, both women looking supremely uncomfortable. Dad turned his gaze back to us. *Girls,* he signed, with a disapproving look on his face. This wasn't something we should watch, we all knew.

And so we turned back to the table, and tried to talk, but our minds were elsewhere, and we ended up finishing up our cups of weak coffee and plates of expensive-looking pastries in an uncomfortable silence.

Miss Strayer came back after a few moments, scooped up her coat, wrapped her scarf around her neck, and slung her messenger bag across her shoulder. She waved. *I have to get going. Thanks again for inviting me.* She looked at me and Rosemary and Dad, her eyes distant above her plastic smile, and walked away. The look on her face had been one of concealed pain, and I realized then that we may have done something very, very wrong.

After she had left, I looked around for Mrs. Perez, who was nowhere to be found.

Every time I closed my eyes, I saw the look on Miss Strayer's face as she walked away from us. All at once, in a wave of understanding as powerful as the ocean waves, or the swells of an orchestra, I understood the thing that had caused so much trouble all those months ago. I knew now how a tree would sabotage another: by accident.

40. fault

AS MISS STRAYER WALKED away, I think that all three of us knew that we had failed. Soon after Miss Strayer left, Fern and Jenna left, and eventually, so did we. We didn't talk much on the car ride, and the silence was so vast and uncomfortable that I almost wished Dad had yelled at us instead. He had gotten a rental car for the day, and the interior smelled so objectionable that the ten-minute ride seemed infinitely longer. This feeling was only exacerbated by the collective understanding of what we had witnessed. Unsaid words hung in the car among the three of us.

When we pulled into the garage, we wordlessly exited the car. I let myself in the house and proceeded to get changed out of my dress and into blue jeans and a sweatshirt that I'd had since fifth grade. Feeling a bit more comfortable, I finally let myself ponder what had happened in the theater lobby.

It obviously had not gone well, but why? Were they still so angry with each other that a civilized conversation was too much to ask? Was there so much more to the story that we didn't know what we were getting ourselves into? The latter seemed more probable. Thinking back, my decision to facilitate this reunion was somewhat reckless, inspired by nothing more than a longing for adventure. I thought maybe I could fix something that had been broken, and maybe there was even something deep down inside me that thought I could bring my mother back, but it was foolish. It was foolish of me to expect anything to come of it, foolish to even try. The plan had backfired, and it was my fault.

I spent much of the remainder of the day alone, not wanting to have to explain anything to anyone. I didn't even have it in me to explain it to myself. I sat in front of the TV, wasting the hours away with the help of a package of stale but edible Oreos and a cup of hot cocoa. Audrey spent the afternoon in her bedroom, as usual. I guessed that we were facing similar moral and emotional dilemmas, but I didn't go in to check on her. Dad had gone into the university to work for a couple hours, so for a while it was just the two of us. And Benjamin. Benjamin the cat, who spent so little time with me, who knew nothing of injustice or the unreasonableness of angry people.

I realized how theatrically tragic my thoughts had become, and inwardly tried to smile at my silliness. I turned my attention back to the television, grabbing another Oreo and absentmindedly breaking it apart.

After a little while, Audrey came out of her room, and sat beside me on the old battered sofa. She grabbed an Oreo and shoved it into her mouth in one bite. She was distressed, and I considered saying something to her, but she seemed to be in one of her more reclusive moods, and so I wordlessly turned the subtitles on the cooking show I was watching, and we watched mindless television for most of the afternoon. It was nice to not have the deadline of the concert hanging over my head, and for a little while, I relaxed.

When Dad came home, we rushed over to the door, motivated by his earlier promise of takeout. We took the brown paper bags containing our dinner from him, and I saw that he looked exhausted. I wondered if something had happened at the university.

We ate in relative silence, commenting on the events of the day only vaguely. I was tired, and ate slowly. Audrey barely touched her food, though. *You okay?* I asked her about halfway through the meal.

She shrugged, not meeting my eyes. After dinner, we went into our respective rooms. I read for a while, but something tugged at the back of my mind, keeping me from focusing on my book. I slipped out the door and went to check on Audrey. As I approached her room, I heard a muffled sound from behind the door, and I hurried in.

My sister was collapsed in a heap on the floor, rocking back and forth, crying softly. I rushed over, crouching next to her. *Audrey.* No response. *Audrey!* Nothing. *Audrey, what's wrong?*

She shook her head. *Can't-*

I sat cross legged on the floor across from her, grabbed her hands and looked her in the eye. *Audrey.*

Finally she looked up at me, disentangling her hands from mine. *My fault,* was all she said.

What's your fault?

She signed a series of seemingly disconnected words. *Trees. . .the root systems. . .sabotage. . .by accident. . . my fault. . .the universe. . .everything splitting and breaking. . .and. . .Benjamin. . .my fault. . .*

I wasn't sure how to handle this one. *Should I get Dad?*

She shook her head emphatically, insistently. *No. No, no, no. My fault.*

Audrey, look at me. She did, but only for a moment. *What is your fault? What are you talking about?*

She fidgeted incoherently with her fingers, with the carpet, with the hem of her shirt, as though trying to find her words. She shook her head again, her hair flopping over her face. *Can't explain.*

My throat tightened. I really hoped something wasn't seriously wrong. *Can you try? Please. If you don't want me to get Dad, you have to tell me now.*

She sat up, her hands continuing to move across the carpet. *Where's Benjamin?*

I sighed. *I thought he was in here.*

Can you go find him?

I sighed again. *Can we just talk?*

She shook her head, her curls flopping in front of her face. She didn't lift a finger to move them out of the way. I didn't see how Benjamin was so crucial to this discussion, but the more pressing issue was leaving Audrey alone. I wasn't sure if I should leave her like this.

She shook her head. *No. Can you please get him? Please. Then we can talk.*

When she got into one of her moods, I knew how stubborn Audrey could be, and so I nervously slipped out of the room to hunt down Benjamin. As I searched, I began to worry more and more. Maybe she had told Dad, but I still had no idea what had happened the night we had come home to Audrey crying, the last time I had seen her like this. I was concerned that it had happened twice in just a couple of months.

I finally found the cat sleeping on top of the whirring clothes dryer, and I scooped him up, hoping he wouldn't be too angry at the interruption. "Come on, buddy, Audrey needs you." At the sound of her name, his ears perked up, and despite the circumstances, I felt a pang of jealousy, an almost imperceptibly small twinge of envy. I squashed it down before I could think about it too much.

With Benjamin nestled in the folds of my sweatshirt, I hurried back to Audrey's room. I found her in the same position I had left her in, slouched on the carpet, staring at the wall. Instinctively, I turned to call for Dad, but I remembered how insistently she had refused that offer. For a moment, I stood in a literal as well as figurative doorway as I contemplated the battle over my loyalty to my sister versus my common sense.

My decision was made for me when Audrey glanced my way, either sensing my presence or, more likely, feeling the vibrations of the floor when I arrived. I stepped the rest of the way into the room, and set Benjamin down on the floor. He scampered over to Audrey, settling down in her lap. She began rhythmically stroking his head, and she became visibly calmer.

I sat down in front of her again, trying to suppress my irritation. *So. What's going on?*

She just stroked the cat's head for a moment, and began to sign, all the while looking at Benjamin rather than me.

You know about parallel universes?

I nodded. *Sort of.* I had heard the term, but had no idea what it meant.

So according to this theory, every time somebody

makes a decision, the universe splits in two. And so there's this one reality where the person made one decision, and another reality where they chose the other option. So there's really like a billion copies of each of us. According to the theory.

Her brown eyes were intense. *Okay. . . .*

And then this guy came up with this theory that something can be dead and alive at the same time. Like there's a moment when someone makes a decision but they don't know it yet, and so the realities are the same for just a little while, where both realities are "real."

I nodded, only vaguely understanding her scientific language. I was a little troubled by the look in her eyes.

So he proposed this experiment with a cat in a box with radioactive substances. So the cat could be dead and alive at the same time.

She stopped, her eyes locked on mine. Suddenly something slid into place in my memory, and I glanced down at Benjamin, who Audrey was still petting. His eyes looked large and innocent compared to the troubled eyes above him, the eyes of my sister. My sister who had been crying on the floor with a cardboard box and a cat.

I inhaled sharply as I realized what had happened that night. But instead of being horrified,

I was oddly calm as I signed to her. *So that's what happened the night of the winter concert.*

She looked relieved, and I understood why. If I had been in her shoes, I wouldn't want to explain any further than that.

I thought that maybe I was missing some vital part of this. *Is that what this is about? Tonight?*

She shrugged. *Sort of.*

I kept looking at her, hoping she'd tell me more but also hoping she wouldn't.

After a moment she continued. *Did you know that trees can sabotage one another?*

I tilted my head to the side. *Sabotage?*

She exhaled slowly. *They use their roots to communicate. They use them to send nutrients and stuff. But they can also. . .use it for. . .other things. Evil.*

Evil?

She shrugged. *Well, the book said sabotage. And then. . .today.*

What do you mean?

With Miss Strayer. And Mrs. Perez. We. . . sabotaged. And it was my fault.

I paused, confused. If anything, I thought, it was *my* fault.

How is that your fault?

She looked down at the carpet, running her

fingers over it. *You wanted so badly to help them. And so did Fern. But I didn't. I never thought it was a good idea and I was going to stop you but I didn't. . .*and she was crying again.

Audrey. . .how is that your fault? If it's anyone's fault, it's mine. If you had said something, I would have stopped.

She shook her head violently. *You don't understand.*

And I didn't. I didn't understand why this was so important, or why it bothered her so much, and I hated that I didn't. I nodded. *I know.*

It's my fault, she said again.

I just sat with her for a while, not saying anything. There were no words that would fix this, I knew. I sat with her while she cried and sat with her when she stopped crying. We sat in silence for what felt like hours.

Was it anyone's fault? If I hadn't invited Miss Strayer, she might have come anyway. The event was open to the public. Miss Strayer and her mother would have to run into another at some point, living in a town as small as Ashton Heights. So was it anyone's fault? I wanted to take the blame, to avoid Fern or Audrey getting in trouble. But as I thought about it, I figured that in reality, it was no one's fault. It had happened, and it needed to be dealt with. But, it did not need to be cried over.

Hey, I signed after a while. I had lost all sense of time, and so it may have been five minutes or five hours; I didn't know or care. *Wanna go for a walk?*

She shrugged. There was a park nearby our house where we used to go a lot with Mom, but hadn't been in a while. *We can go walking in the park.*

She didn't look happy about it, but in the end, she relented.

And so we went for a walk in the park. It was funny how a "walk in the park" was usually used to describe something easy or mindless. Sometimes a walk in the park is difficult, sometimes it is easy, and sometimes it is neither. Sometimes it is just what you need.

41. spotLights

A FEW DAYS AFTER the concert, after which Rosemary gave Dad a watered-down version of the story, I gave my presentation to the entire ninth grade. In the beginning of the assembly, I sat in a bit of a nervous trance in the back of the auditorium that looked like it had cost several thousand dollars less than the one at Rosemary's school.

I watched as each student presented his or her project, only registering minimal information about their chosen topics. There was an interpreter for me, but I wasn't paying much attention. My name was fairly early in the alphabet, so I was able to get it over with.

The translator signed my name as Mrs.

Alvarez called on me.

    I slowly walked up to the podium. *Hello,* I signed. There were bright lights shining on me, which obstructed my view of the audience. *I'm Audrey Cooper.* The interpreter translated to spoken word as I signed. *I chose to do my project on tree communication. You see, trees use their roots for far more than just absorbing water and nutrients. They use them to communicate. An older tree, known as a mother tree, can communicate to other trees over a distance of up to seven miles.*

    As I went into the details of the presentation, including the Robert Frost poem, my tree experiment, and my analysis of the number e, I gained confidence. Since I had never had the opportunity to speak in front of so many people before, I was a bit nervous, but talking to a theater full of vague, faraway faces was significantly easier than talking to a small group of people, all of whom were looking at me.

    Trees use their roots, above all, to communicate. Their language is far below the surface, and perhaps hard for most of us to understand, but it is there, if we are willing to see it. Through this system, a tree can theoretically transport a message to another tree miles and miles away.

This recent discovery of the linguistic capabilities of trees can teach us many things. For one, not all communicative language is verbal.

And I smiled. For real.

And more importantly, everything is deeply connected, far more so than we ever thought before. We can't see or hear these connections, but we can observe their effects. And that is the most fascinating part, I think, of being able to live in this world. We get to see all the choices we make in silence play out in ways we never thought possible. And we share this experience with the trees.

The project went far faster than I had expected. As I took a small bow and walked away from the podium, I was grateful to be out of the glare of the spotlight, but a strange, small part of me was disappointed to leave.

That same day, Fern and Rosemary met me at school to walk to the library. Our meetings at the Ashton Heights Public Library were becoming a weekly thing. It was small, but it was nice to have something like that to look forward to.

Hey guys, I signed as they met me on the sidewalk in front of the ugly square building that was Ashton Heights High School. We walked down the street, passing all sorts of people, all of whom had roots, I thought, stretching far beyond our vision.

We arrived at the beautiful Victorian-style library in about ten minutes. The shelf-lined walls and comfortable chairs were a welcome relief from the harsh fluorescent lights and blaringly bright checkered floor of the high school.

So, Fern signed as we sat down at our usual table near the window. Her signing was quickly progressing, and I secretly suspected that Rosemary was behind that. *How'd it go today?*

I nodded. *Pretty well.* I told them about the spotlights, and how I couldn't see anyone in the theater.

Rosie laughed. *You like that? I hate when I can't see who I'm performing for!*

I shrugged. *Makes it easier, I guess.*

Fern chimed in with a laugh. *You guys are so different. Are you sure you're twins?*

We both looked at her, and laughed when we realized we were giving her the exact same *"are you sure about that"* expression. Fern threw back her head and laughed. *Never mind.*

Rosemary's head jerked up suddenly, looking at something behind me and Fern, towards the door. *Don't turn around,* Rosemary signed suddenly, with small, subtle hand movements. *Mrs. Perez.*

My eyes widened. Despite my sister's warning, I instinctively turned around to look. Mrs. Perez had just walked in the library. She stood near the doorway, looking around as though searching for someone. She was wearing a long floral skirt, and a wide-brimmed hat, looking like the epitome of fashion one hundred years ago. She looked a little unsure as she scanned the library.

Fern and I hastily turned back to Rosemary as Mrs. Perez turned towards us. Rosemary began talking again, about what she had learned in school today, and what books she was reading, and random bits of unimportant things like that, just to look like we were engaged in a deep conversation.

Mrs. Perez sat down at a table on the other side of the library. A few moments later, Rosemary's eyes widened even further. We turned around, trying to be inconspicuous, but forgot all about being subtle as we watched Miranda Strayer walk in the door.

42. narrating

WHEN I SAW MISS Miranda Strayer walk in the library doors, I audibly gasped. Thankfully, she didn't seem to have heard me.

I took a deep breath, wondering what would happen next. Audrey and Fern turned back to the table, and we tried to talk about normal things while I watched the drama unfold behind Audrey and Fern's backs. I signed what was happening to them as it happened, like the narrator of a story.

Miss Strayer is sitting down at Mrs. Perez's table. . .they're talking. . .Miss Strayer is crying. . .they're talking again. . .now Mrs. Perez is crying. . .they're talking. . .they're standing up. . .Miss Strayer's walking around the table. . .now they're hugging. . .and crying. . .and they're leaving. . .

When I wasn't watching their table, I was watching Audrey's and Fern's faces. Fern was smiling as I narrated, but Audrey's expression betrayed something I couldn't quite place. She looked a bit. . .unsure, but there was something else.

There's something in literature called narrative voice. This refers to the tone that the narrator uses, the reliability of the narrator, and the narrator's proximity to the events of the story. I wondered how this story would play out if it was narrated by someone else, like Miss Strayer, or Dad, or even Benjamin. I hoped I was a reliable narrator.

When Miss Strayer and Mrs. Perez left the library, we all watched out the window as they talked, and eventually disappeared around a corner. *Wow,* I signed slowly.

Fern shook her head. "What just happened?" she asked.

Audrey gave a small smile. *Root networks,* she signed mysteriously.

Fern tilted her head to the side, looking bewildered. *Huh?*

You know, how tree roots can communicate? The subterranean connections?

I shook my head, a grin spreading across my face. *And you say you're not a poet.*

ELISE STANKUS

part 4. spring

"She turned to the sunlight
And shook her yellow head,
And whispered to her neighbor:
'Winter is dead.' "

-A.A Milne

ELISE STANKUS

43. symbiOsis

SYMBIOSIS REFERS TO A RELATIONSHIP between two organisms in which both creatures benefit from the relationship. A classic example of this is mycorrhizal fungi.

Mycorrhizae are small fungi that attach themselves to tree roots. They absorb nutrients and water from the soil and pass them onto the tree. The mycorrhizae is able to benefit from this by keeping some of the nutrients and water for itself, like a toll.

In addition to collecting essential nutrients for the tree, the mycorrhizae are extremely important in the root communication network. They are able to pass nutrients or chemical messages to the mycorrhizae of the roots of other trees. In a way, they are the postal service of the trees.

I was thinking about symbiosis as Miss Strayer and Mrs. Perez walked away from the library that day. Sometimes trees cannot communicate without the help of other organisms. The great underground postal service only works because the trees and the soil and the mycorrhizae are all working together to make it happen.

Maybe that was the way with people, too. We were all connected, but sometimes we needed someone else to show us that. The tree roots are intertwined, but we need the mycorrhizae sometimes to show us how the connection works.

44. beginnings

MY NEXT VIOLIN LESSON was a few weeks after we had seen Miss Strayer and Mrs. Perez in the library. Those weeks had passed rather uneventfully. But needless to say, I was a bit nervous about how the lesson would go. I hadn't talked to Miss Strayer since the day of the concert, and I wondered if she would even mention it. I wasn't sure which would be more uncomfortable: Miss Strayer trying to discuss it, or avoiding the topic altogether.

After the concert, it was as though we were entering into a new beginning of some sort. The show was over; orchestra practice was less intense. Audrey's project was done. The second semester of school was under way, and it seemed like the most difficult part of freshman year had passed with the passing of midterms.

In the old stories, beginnings always started with "once upon a time." My favorite stories started with this cliche, but I have never liked it all that much. For one thing, beginnings were always more complicated than that, just like endings were always more complicated than a simple "happily ever after." A lot of times, you don't realize you're beginning something until it's already begun. As I thought about my lesson the next day, lying awake in bed, I wondered whether I was walking into a beginning or an ending.

I asked Audrey if she would come with me, and she agreed. Miss Strayer always enjoyed it when she came, and I would be glad to have another person there if Miss Strayer wanted to explain anything.

I woke up early that morning, thinking hard. The sun was just rising, and I was the only one awake in the house, which I had always loved. It was that time in the morning when most people were still asleep, and there was a strange hush over the neighborhood. I stepped outside for a moment. The air always seemed fresher, brisker in the morning. It was refreshing; I hadn't spent much time outside lately, with school and orchestra taking up much of my time. I thought about the night I had lain outside under the stars while Dad comforted Audrey, after my winter concert, when Audrey had almost attempted her "experiment." That felt like it had happened so long ago, though it was really only a couple of months ago. We had all changed so much since then.

Sighing, I slipped back inside, as the icy breeze had become too much to bear in just my pajama pants and sweatshirt.

I wondered if Miss Strayer had any idea that we knew what had happened. Just as I thought that, I took it back. We *hadn't* known what happened. We had set it up, but we still knew only the bare minimum of the situation. We knew that Miss Strayer had left. Whether she ran away, moved away, or something else was still a big unknown. We knew that she and her mother had not been on speaking terms for several years. Had it been since high school since they talked? Had they been estranged in the first place because of Miss Strayer's leaving? Or was it something else?

I became more and more worried as I thought about it. What if she knew that I had set it up? It had seemed like they had at least partially patched things up in the library a few weeks ago, but what if they hadn't? What if Miss Strayer blamed me for the incident in the theater lobby?

As I fixed my bagel, I thought about Audrey and Fern. I would have never expected the two of them to be friends, but ever since our first meeting in the library, they seemed to click. Anything could happen, I thought, and realized that there was something good that came out of all this, after all.

I poured myself a glass of orange juice, and jumped when I heard a sharp sound from the other side of the kitchen. A splatter of orange juice fell to the floor as I abruptly turned to see what it was.

I turned around to find Audrey fixing herself a bowl of cereal. She was normally a late sleeper, and so I was surprised to see her. I laughed at her expression. *You scared me!* I signed, mostly good-naturedly, but with a bit of irritation at my lost orange juice.

She laughed. *Sorry. I woke up early and figured I'd just come and eat.*

I nodded. *Me too.*

I looked out the window. Spring was just around the corner, and you could almost see the buds on the trees just lurking below the surface, getting ready to emerge. It was that time of year when nature was just about ready to explode with color after the dull winter. It was rather peaceful.

We sat down at the kitchen table. The sun had just risen recently, and Dad was still asleep. We ate quickly and quietly.

After a while, Dad came out from his room and sleepily fixed his coffee and cereal. I got ready for my lesson and the three of us hurried out the door.

As soon as we got in the car, Dad rubbed his eyes. "Okay. Who's ready to tell me what happened after the concert?"

Audrey and I shared a surprised glance. No one had mentioned the event since it happened. Honestly I had my doubts about how much of it Dad had picked up on.

We were silent.

"Look, girls, I could tell you had something to do with that. I know you. You invited Miss Strayer, right?"

I nodded. "Yes, but-" I cut off abruptly, not sure how to continue.

"So Mrs. Perez is Miss Strayer's mother, yes?" Dad's voice was firm and to the point.

My eyes widened. "How could you tell?"

"I taught Miranda in college, remember?"

We nodded. Somehow we had forgotten that along the way.

"Miranda wasn't talking to her mother in college, but her mom stopped by occasionally, to check on her, I suppose. I met her a few times. I recognized her in the car that day, in Miss Strayer's neighborhood, though she obviously didn't recognize me. I suspected something was up because she was just sitting there and didn't want directions."

He sighed. "So, how much of that had you figured out already?"

Audrey looked grim. *All of it,* she signed, slowly.

"And more," I added. I was surprised by how small and weak my voice sounded.

He just stared at us for a few moments, looking from me to my sister and back to me.

He started the car just as I thought I would definitely be late to my lesson, and we pulled out of the driveway. I was glad he hadn't demanded more details.

We had gotten the minivan back a few days prior and though it had cost a small fortune to repair, it was nice to have it back.

Maybe that was a sign that this was a beginning, not an ending.

45. the uniVerse

AS WE DROVE ALONG the highway to Miss Strayer's house, I thought about my mother. I wondered about the choices that had directly or indirectly resulted in her death. Maybe it was the other driver's choice to get up in the morning. Maybe it was my choice to ask Mommy something before she left, so she was a little late. Maybe it was even her choice to go at all.

It was mysterious, like the story about Miss Strayer and Mrs. Perez. Perhaps even more mysterious.

As we drove along the gently sloping highway, I thought about all the choices that had taken place in order for me to be here. All the parallel universes in which other Audreys were doing different things.

Something occurred to me, suddenly, as I looked out the window from the backseat, watching the world whiz by in a greenish blur. I saw a flash of images in my mind, and something clicked into place, like that one puzzle piece that you lost under the table finally sliding into the bigger picture. I saw myself lifting a kitten out of a cardboard box, and my sister playing the violin, and two sisters looking coldly at each other from across a table in a public library. I saw Miss Strayer scrawling notes on pages ripped out of a textbook before she left, and her mother crying as a lawyer in a pinstripe suit told her, "There's nothing we can do." I saw my father shuttling my sister and I all over town, and I saw my mother smiling. I saw a whole lot of choices being made, and a whole lot of people moving on with their lives nonetheless. I saw a world breaking, and I saw a world healing itself.

Maybe it wasn't our *choices* that made the universe split. Maybe it was just the universe doing its thing. Maybe it was just the natural order of things, like a tree branch splitting in two in order to get more nutrients. It was like the mystery novels my mother used to read, the kind where the protagonist is tossed around like loose change at a passing whim of the author, while somehow still managing to save the day.

But maybe the mystery is just part of living in this world. The trees in the forest don't know when a lightning storm will strike and knock one of them down. They don't know when the lumberjacks will come, or when a deaf girl in a faraway town will research them in a dark library, learning their ways, only to find out that some things will never be known. But perhaps they didn't need to know. They didn't need to know these things to transport nutrients to their young, or to keep a stump alive with water and sugar and whatever else they used to keep the dead alive for a little bit longer.

Despite all this, I thought, it still wasn't fair. It wasn't fair that some trees could sustain the small spark of life in a rotting stump. It wasn't fair that Miss Strayer's mother came back and mine did not.

But perhaps that was not the point. I closed my eyes as the world whizzed past, a big, breaking, healing, beautiful universe.

46. pouring out

WE ARRIVED AT Miss Strayer's house just a few minutes late. Dad dropped us off by the door and we hesitantly stepped up to the front door. Miss Strayer was waiting for us, with her hair down, her thin beaded braids hanging loosely around her face. Her eyes were tired, but she smiled at us and beckoned us inside. We walked through the color-dappled foyer into the living room. "Why don't you girls go on into the music room? I'll be right in."

She disappeared into the kitchen and Audrey and I went down the still-cluttered hallway and into the yellow light of the music room. Since the sun was on the other side of the house, it wasn't shining directly in the window but the light from several lamps scattered throughout the room gave it a warm glow.

All the musical instruments seemed to be in their rightful spots, but something seemed out of place. I couldn't put my finger on it until Audrey pointed at the wall opposite the grand piano, where there was a blank square. It took me a moment to remember, but then I realized that it was the spot where the picture of Mrs. Perez had been hanging.

Before I could say anything, Miss Strayer came rushing into the room. "So sorry!" she exclaimed. "I had to finish something in the other room."

"So glad to see you, Audrey," she said, "I love it when you come and listen."

Randomly, I remembered my conversation with Audrey in which she told me she liked the glare of the spotlight, and I wondered if Miss Strayer was the kind of person who likes to see her audience or the kind of person who finds comfort in the blinding lights. I suspected she was like Audrey, but I didn't ask her.

"So, Rosemary, let's see that violin," she said cheerily, sitting down on her easy chair in front of the piano. I pulled my instrument out of the case, wondering if she was even going to address what had happened.

We played a few duets that we had been practicing, pieces that took advantage of Miss Strayer's wide array of musical instruments but showcased my violin as the main instrument. She let Audrey play a little piano to accompany me, showing her which notes to play and when. I was impressed by how quickly she picked it up.

Before I knew it, the lesson was over. She stood up from her chair and opened her mouth to say something. She closed it and pursed her lips, thinking. "You know what?" she asked, trying to disguise the nervous tinge to her normally cheerful voice. "Why don't you girls go and sit in the living room for a minute? I'd like to talk to you two for a bit, if you don't mind." She said it with the tone of voice somebody used when they were thinking about saying something for a long time, but wanted it to seem as though they had just thought of it.

Audrey and I looked at each other and shrugged. "Sure," I said. We walked out into the living room, sitting down tentatively on the colorfully patched-up couch. My hands nervously fluttered like little birds as I signed to my sister. *Do you think she's going to explain everything? Or want us to?*

Audrey shrugged. *Maybe. What if she's mad at us?*

She has no way of knowing that we know any of it. As I said it, I realized how cunning, how deceptive, that sounded. I asked again the question I'd been wondering about for weeks. *Audrey, was it bad that we kept searching for information about this? Do you think we went too far?*

She exhaled slowly, not meeting my eyes. *I really don't know.*

Before she could say anymore, Miss Strayer emerged from the music room and sat down in a chair facing us. She seemed a little awkward, as though she wasn't sure how to begin the conversation.

So. Her signing was still pretty clumsy, so she soon switched to spoken English, and I absentmindedly interpreted for Audrey. "I imagine that you're probably wondering what happened a few weeks ago. After the concert."

Audrey and I must have looked pretty uncomfortable, because she backtracked, misinterpreting our discomfort. "Don't worry - you're not in trouble. You did nothing wrong."

You have no idea, I thought.

She continued, looking down at her hands,

which were folded in her lap. "Um. So your teacher, Rosemary - Mrs. Perez - she's. . .well, she's my mother."

She turned towards us, and we did our best to display the facades of surprise that we knew she was expecting. Only then did she continue. "She and I - well, we, um, went a long time without speaking. We haven't seen each other in a long time. And - you saw what happened."

Realizing that she was done with her story, I gritted my teeth as I turned towards Audrey, who nodded infinitesimally. I took a deep breath. "Miss Strayer, we - well, me. It was me. I, um. You see, I happened to overhear a conversation with Mrs. Perez - your mom - it was by accident, I promise, but. . .I was able to figure that out." I knew I was rambling, and I knew I probably wasn't making much sense. But Miss Strayer seemed to understand, at least the parts of the story I was explaining. I wasn't ready to divulge the whole thing, but I figured she should know some of it.

She nodded, slowly taking in my rambling speech. "I see," she said, after a few moments of painful silence.

"I'm sorry," I said in a small voice.

She looked surprised. "Why are you sorry?"

"I just - I went looking for trouble, and it seems that I found it."

"Don't you ever apologize for that, Rosemary. There's such a thing as good trouble, you know."

I gave her a small smile.

She tilted her head to the side with a puzzled expression as something occurred to her. "So. . .how much do you know, exactly?" she asked, her voice sounding a bit nervous but retaining its usual warmth. I could tell she wasn't mad, and something inside me relaxed.

"Well. . .do you want to just tell us what happened?" After a moment, I shook my head. "Sorry, that sounded really rude. I didn't mean it that way, I just. . .you don't have to tell us if you're not ready, but. . ."

To my surprise, she laughed. "Believe it or not, it just might be a weight off my shoulders to explain it. Do you really want to know?"

Audrey and I turned to each other, surprised. I looked back at Miss Strayer and nodded, slowly. "Only if you don't mind."

She sat back in her chair and looked up at the ceiling, relaxing for the first time that day. "Good Lord," she began, "where do I even start?"

Audrey and I sat back as well, sinking into the already-sunken cushions of the navy-blue couch. Suddenly, I noticed the photo that had been missing from the music room. The grainy photo of mother and daughter hung above the doorway to the kitchen.

Miss Strayer took a deep breath, and her eyes became distant, like the eyes of old storytellers in the movies, when they disappear into their memories. "Well, I may or may not have told you this, but I went to St. Michael's, too, Rosemary. Although, you probably have figured that out already."

I nodded hesitantly.

"Right. So I guess I should backtrack a little. I never knew my dad, and once my mom came from Costa Rica with my twin brother and me when we were toddlers, she had kind of come to terms with the fact that we would never know our dad. I don't know where he is, by the way. I don't even know if he's alive. But anyway, when my mom realized that she'd probably be a single mom her whole life, she decided that we'd better make some good money to make up for that. She always had this ideal of the "American Dream." Where a parent can make a better life for her children. But her idea of a "better life" was not exactly the same as ours. A doctor or a lawyer, she said. She had our whole lives planned out." Miss Strayer paused and sighed.

"But I did not want to be a doctor or a lawyer. I know it sounds petty, but I could not bring myself to do work I hated just for money, and I guess I. . .wanted to live my own life, if that makes sense. I wasn't just trying to get out of working and living a normal life. I just didn't want the life my mom wanted for me. I wanted to be a musician, obviously, and at the risk of sounding like a stereotypical artist, I will say that there was nothing anyone could do to keep me from that. And my mother eventually said that she would not, and I quote, 'put a single cent towards my college education unless you go to medical or law school.' She said other things, too - worse things - that all added up to our estrangement."

She paused again, looking up towards the ceiling. I knew that look well. It was the expression of someone who was trying their best to hide the fact that they were desperately trying not to cry.

"I was a pretty stubborn teenager, I guess," she said, her voice breaking slightly. "Like you girls. Except far less wise." She chuckled, but it seemed forced. "Pretty reckless, too, I suppose, and hardheaded. So in the end, I. . .I left. I left the house one day after leaving a note for my mom. And that was it. I didn't even say goodbye. I had never really had your typical touchy-feely mother-daughter relationship, so I'm sorry to say it wasn't hard. I just walked out. Just a note. Well, a few notes, come to think of it. You might laugh, but I actually had a whole system of hidden notes at school to tell my friends about my plan."

Audrey shook her head, entirely serious. *We wouldn't laugh*, she signed. I could see that Miss Strayer understood, and she and I both burst out laughing.

Miss Strayer looked at the both of us. "You found them, didn't you? You found my notes." She shook her head, chuckling. We nodded, and she began to laugh harder. "Of course you did! Man, you girls are clever."

Audrey shrugged, ever the detail-oriented realist. *Actually, it was Rosie and Fern who found the notes.*

Miss Strayer tilted her head. "Fern?" I could tell she didn't remember her from the concert. I supposed she had other things on her mind then.

"She's my friend - our friend - from St.

Michael's. She sat next to me in the orchestra. And at our table at the concert. You were talking to her sister Jenna."

She slapped her forehead. "Of course! I remembered Jenna from St. Mike's. Apparently she didn't know me too well while I was there, but I always thought she was pretty cool." Miss Strayer chuckled again, and I could tell that despite the grim topic, she was enjoying her little stroll down memory lane. "So, Fern is Jenna Reynolds' sister. Funny, she never mentioned a sister. . ."

I remembered Fern's uneasy look when Jenna sat next to her during our second trip to the library, and then I looked over at my own sister, who was watching Miss Strayer intently. "So you and Fern found my notes. Did you go to the library on September 7th at 3:00?" she asked with a smile.

I nodded, and a grin spread across my face. "We were so confused when nobody showed up!"

Miss Strayer shrugged. "That's because they were - oh, let's see - ten years old? And by then I was long gone. . ."

Audrey looked up at her. *I shall be gone,* she signed.

Miss Strayer nodded, remembering the poem. She paused, and I felt like I had to keep her on track if she was going to finish the story.

"What happened next?"

"Well. . .I went and stayed with a friend for a while, and I found myself a job, and played some gigs. Looking back, I'm not really sure how I did it, but. . . .somehow I managed, I guess. I was able to rent a super cheap apartment after a few months, and I continued to work. Eventually I decided I didn't really want to be associated with my family anymore, so I changed my name. Strayer was an old family name, and it seemed to be. . .fit for the situation."

I shook my head. "Wow. . .what happened to your brother?" I remembered her comment, all those months ago when I first met her, that she didn't get along with him.

"Well. Colin went to law school, and moved to New York City. Last I heard, he was pretty successful. Momma's little boy," she added with a scoff. I pictured Mrs. Perez's desk at school. There was only one photograph on it, the same one that hung above Miss Strayer's doorway.

"And so I got my GED, and eventually got a music scholarship to the university, so I could go to college, even after dropping out of high school. And your dad was my history professor, as I'm sure you know. I didn't speak to my mother for about eight years - until the other day. And you know the rest. And. . . well, that's about it. That's my story."

She sighed, sitting back in her chair. "Now, why don't you two tell me about how you found all that out." Her eyes were curious, and more relaxed than before.

Audrey and I looked at each other, silently asking each other who would start. I wasn't sure even *where* to start, but thankfully my sister began signing before I could think of anything.

If a tree falls in the forest, it does make a sound, you know.

I looked at her abruptly. *What?*

It makes a sound. Even if there's nobody there to hear it. She was looking at us expectantly, as though this was something completely relevant to the current conversation.

Okay. . .What does that have to do with anything? I was a little annoyed at the complete change of topic.

She shrugged. *You know, the whole parallel universe thing?*

I sighed. *Audrey. . .*

She cut me off. *No, just listen to me. I'm getting there.*

I nodded, taken aback. *Sure, go ahead.* I glanced at Miss Strayer, who was obviously not following the conversation, but she looked intrigued.

Audrey took a deep breath, and continued. *So when a tree falls, or dies, or is cut down - it doesn't really matter - the other trees around it can tell. Because they communicate through their roots, and leaves, and stuff. They know. But the crazy thing is that they can keep the dead tree alive for years after it falls, or is cut down, or whatever. So it's just a stump, but the trees around it are still sending water and nutrients to the stump. So the tree is dead, but the stump is still alive.*

Miss Strayer smiled. *That's amazing.*

Audrey nodded vigorously. She briefly explained the cat experiment thing that she had studied, and I was aware of how crazy it all sounded, but Miss Strayer seemed genuinely interested. Maybe *crazy* was a relative term.

I listened to my sister. *And Schrodinger thought that if the box was still closed, then the cat was both dead and alive at the same time, but there was no way to know, because once you open the box, the realities split, and the cat is EITHER alive or dead, not both.*

Stretching her fingers, Audrey continued. *So the trees have kind of solved the problem that physicists have been trying to solve for decades.*

"Wow. . ." Miss Strayer breathed. "That's pretty incredible."

Slightly irritated, I tried to direct her story back to Miss Strayer and her mom and the notes, and Fern. *So what does that have to do with the story?* I signed as kindly as I could.

Miss Strayer looked at me sharply. "Rosemary," was all she said, but her voice was icy, and I was taken aback. She nodded towards Audrey.

My sister went on with her wild ramble. If she had seen the look Miss Strayer had given me, she didn't react. *So all the trees in the world, or at least on the continent, are somehow connected through their roots. Under the ground. And they speak a language that we can't see, or hear, or feel.*

She paused, fidgeting with the hem of her sweatshirt. *The sound of trees. . .*

So Rosemary and Fern found the notes, and oddly enough, neither of them told me until weeks later. She shot a look in my direction, but it was more playful than accusatory. I was surprised by the abrupt change in the tone of her story, but I trusted her.

We were in the mall one day, and I found this

poem that I really liked, that I had read at school, and we went back to the bookstore that we had found it in, and there you were!

And Rosemary said that we should go see if it was the same book, and so she went and asked you, and you remember that, so I don't have to tell you about how that went.

It was funny. I couldn't remember the last time Audrey had talked for this long. Usually she used the minimum amount of words to get a message across, but here she was, spouting the complex, multi-faceted story complete with details.

And then, Rosemary and Fern found your other note a few weeks later, the one in the textbook in the library. And then eventually they found you in an old yearbook. That was when we realized that you were Miranda. And then we went to the coffee shop and heard the barista talking to you on the phone. She stopped here. We hadn't heard her talk about him yet.

We both looked expectantly at Miss Strayer. She looked slightly uncomfortable. I opened my mouth to tell her that she didn't have to tell us, but before I could say anything, she began talking.

"Well," she said. "I suppose I should've mentioned him when I told you everything else. He's. . .well, that's a bit complicated. I met Jacob in college, a few years after I started living on my own. We were both pretty reckless, and so the summer before our junior year in college, he proposed. And I said yes."

I thought of the ring that Audrey had seen on Miss Strayer's finger at the concert. I glanced down at her hand now, but she wasn't wearing it.

She caught my eye, and looked down at her hand too. "We never got married." she said. "Technically, we're still engaged, but. . .I hadn't spoken to him in a while before that day when I guess you overheard our conversation." She was smiling somewhat mischievously. "You girls happen to overhear a lot, don't you?"

I jumped to our defense. "It was by accident, I swear. Every time. After a while, we started looking for clues, but we never purposefully eavesdropped."

"Every time?" I could tell that she was teasing us, and I relaxed. She believed me.

Audrey spoke up. *Root networks*, she signed with a faraway look on her face.

Miss Strayer smiled. *You may be right. The connections go pretty deep, don't they?*

Audrey nodded, and I watched them, bewildered.

Miss Strayer cleared her throat. I wondered if she thought she might have told us too much. "So, what happened next?" she asked. I suspected that she was purposefully turning the conversation away from this Jacob person.

Audrey continued, still on a roll. *So somewhere along the line - I don't quite remember when - we saw Mrs. Perez - your mom - in her car on a street parallel to this one. Just sitting in her car.*

Miss Strayer's expression changed, and I guessed that this part was new to her.

We thought she was lost, so we stopped, and I thought she looked oddly familiar, but I couldn't think of any reason why I might have seen her before. And Rosemary couldn't either.

Our dad asked if she needed directions, and introduced himself. She didn't need directions, which was weird. We went home and I told Rosemary that I recognized her, and she probably thought I was crazy.

I looked at my sister, expecting a playful expression, but she was entirely serious. It was odd to hear the story chronicled from her side. I had never thought about it that way, and I never for one moment thought that she was crazy. But she had already moved on to the next part.

And. . .once we knew all this, Rosemary wanted

to. . . Audrey glanced at me, and I gave her a small nod, giving her permission to share this part. A part of me wanted to keep it to myself, but in a way it was somewhat of a relief to get all this out in the open.

Rosemary wanted to make sure that the two of you were reunited again.

She stopped suddenly, and the two of us looked at Miss Strayer, wondering how she would react to this. Her eyes widened a little, and to our surprise, began to well up with tears. She smiled at us. I looked at Audrey. This was not what we were expecting. I had assumed that she might get mad at me, but I had not expected her to cry. I couldn't tell if this was better or worse.

Audrey continued hesitantly. *Her intentions were only good, I promise. She wanted. . .she wanted to see a family made whole again.*

Miss Strayer smiled as a tear ran down her cheek. "Oh, girls," she started, her voice small. I knew now that she understood. I let out a long breath, relieved that someone understood at last. "I met your mother once, you know."

I perked up. "Really?"

She nodded, a grin spreading across her face. "She came to a university event once. Well, I'm sure she went a lot, but there was one when I ended up talking to her for a long time. She asked what I did, and I said I was a musician. She told me that she was a poet, and we spent the whole evening talking about the arts, and how music and literature are so deeply connected."

Audrey and I nodded appreciatively.

"And then I went to a poetry reading once. I think it was about Emily Dickinson. Local poets came and read their own work inspired by Dickinson, as well as Emily's work. Your mom was there. She read some beautiful poems. Very talented. And smart, too."

I smiled when she called the poet "Emily," just like Mom always had.

Something occurred to me. "Wait," I said, my face becoming grim and serious again. "When was this reading?"

She looked taken aback, her eyes widening behind her glasses. "Let's see - five years ago maybe? I was a senior in college."

I did a quick calculation.

"That was the last one," I whispered.

Miss Strayer's face fell. "I'm so sorry," she said.

I nodded. "Thanks."

We fell into silence again. Something occurred to me, and I laughed. "Wait." I glanced down at my watch. "Is Dad here? Has he been waiting for us all this time?"

Miss Strayer chuckled, looking guilty. "I gave him a quick call before we started talking. I said you two would be a little late. I wanted to be sure I was able to talk to you before you left. Is there anything else you'd like to tell me?" she added.

"Well. . ." I hadn't said much during the conversation, and there was one more thing I wanted to add. "I invited you to the concert because I knew that your mother would be there. It wasn't Audrey's idea, or Fern's. It was mine. So I'm sorry."

She shook her head, the beads in her braids clinking together like a wind chime. "Please don't apologize for that, Rosemary. Really. Someone had to do it."

I smiled. "And we saw you in the library. And I think that's it."

She nodded. "I thought I saw you in the library." She shook her head again, as though angry with herself. "I'm sorry to burden you girls with all this, but I thought you had the right to know."

"It's okay," I said. "We won't tell anyone.

Right, Audrey?"

I looked over at my sister, whose head was tilted to the side, her curls spilling off her shoulders, a puzzled expression on her face.

What about the poems? She asked.

Miss Strayer matched Audrey's confused expression. "The poems?"

Audrey nodded. *On the notes?*

I had momentarily forgotten about the poems in the chaos of things. We had spent so much time searching for them, and I was just realizing now that Miss Strayer hadn't explained them.

She twirled a dark beaded braid around her finger. *What about them?*

I chuckled. "Everything. Why did you choose those poems? To write your notes on?"

She shook her head. "I didn't. Those were just the papers that the teacher had handed out that day. There's no significance, other than the fact that they were on the same page in the textbook. And then the last line - 'I shall be gone' - seemed relevant, so I underlined it." She shrugged, as though this was a fact of little importance.

Audrey and I gaped at her, and she laughed nervously. "What?"

We looked at each other, and back at Miss

Strayer. Eventually, I broke the silence. "It was *nothing?* There was no significance to those two poems?"

She shook her head slowly, still not understanding the significance of this.

I went on, laughing a little to disguise the anger that was inexplicably blooming up in me. "We spent so long trying to figure those out!" I exclaimed. "We must've searched through a hundred poetry books to try and figure out the meanings!"

I watched Miss Strayer as she absorbed this information. She looked me in the eye. "And do you really think that time was wasted?"

I sputtered. "Do I - I - yes, I think it was wasted!" I wasn't quite sure why I was getting so upset about this, but it had come to mean a lot to me, and I wasn't ready to let go of it so quickly. Miss Strayer saw what was happening.

"Rosemary." I looked up at her, and relaxed my hands, which I had inadvertently balled into tight fists.

"Rosemary, look me in the eye and tell me that you learned nothing from doing that."

And I wanted to.

I wanted to yell at her and tell her that I had

been looking into the poems to get to know my dead mother and make a friend and maybe even to try to do something good for the world, but it had been for nothing. I wanted to look her in the eye and say that it was wasted time.

But I couldn't. I took a breath, staring at my black sneakers, which seemed hilariously out of place against the backdrop of Miss Strayer's colorful shaggy carpet. Miss Strayer's similarly colorful slipper slid over and tapped my foot. I reluctantly looked up at her.

"Rosemary. I get it. And I'm sorry."

I nodded, though I wasn't sure what exactly she was apologizing for. It was enough.

She nodded, cleared her throat, and then hesitated. "I know you probably need to get going, but one more thing to close the story." She glanced at her watch. "In approximately five hours, I will be going to my mom's house. For dinner. To - to straighten some things out."

I couldn't help grinning, even after my recent anger.

Miss Strayer stood up, and so did Audrey and I. "Tree roots can be so hopelessly tangled sometimes, can't they?"

We let out a collective sigh, and started to

laugh, all three of us wiping away tears. The last remaining fragments of tension in the room evaporated as we laughed. Miss Strayer held out her arms, and we each gave her a hug. "Thanks so much, girls," she whispered.

47. flowErs

AFTER THAT DAY at Miss Strayer's, I started noticing things. Like the little flowers near the end of our driveway. It had been flower season for some time, but I had not been looking for things like that. Maybe Dad had been right, when he said that I spent too much time in my head.

Besides being beautiful, flowers serve a very important purpose. By allowing bees and other creatures to pollinate, flowers help trees to grow. And to create more trees. Helping to create a strong, complex, tangled, beautiful language beneath the soil.

There's a school of thought in philosophy called solipsism. This states that the self is the only part of the world that can be known. I used to find this idea comforting, for if the rest of the world could never be known, then maybe it was not as frighteningly real as it seemed. It was as though I lived in a movie. I was not the director of the movie, but I was myself in a cast of characters.

There were things, I was learning, that made me glad that I was not living in a movie. There were things outside my head that made it worthwhile. Perhaps I was an actor sometimes, at other times a stagehand, and at others something else. But never the director. And that was okay. There were flowers that I could have never imagined, had I been directing it all.

I noticed things other than the flowers too. Like how Benjamin only responds to his name in the afternoon. And how Rosemary's violin practice always seemed to go better in the morning. And how Dad often forgot to make coffee on Saturdays. I didn't know how or why or even if these things mattered at all, but they were all new to me, and in a way, they were like flowers blooming all over.

The weird thing about solipsism is that it indicates that there is nothing outside the mind that can be known, not that it is not real. It means that I will never be able to know if what exists outside my mind truly exists, *not* that it is not real. Solipsism allows for the beauty of not knowing, the beauty in mystery.

But, I am learning, there are things much more beautiful than that.

48. roots: part two

TREES DON'T WASTE ANYTHING. Like the people of long ago, trees know how to use everything available to them. Nothing that trees do, or consume, or absorb, is wasted. Their roots absorb water, and nutrients, and they use it all. What they are not able to use goes to the mycorrhizae, the fungi that help the roots absorb water.

So every drop of water, every ounce of the tree's energy, goes toward something good. Even the nutrients transported to a dying tree help fertilize the soil. But more importantly, tree roots can hold light. There are particles in tree roots, called phytochromes, which can sense light. The tree can send light energy down to the roots, allowing the roots to effectively communicate with the parts of the tree that are above the ground. Even a thing as simple as light is never wasted.

One day in late May, the week before school let out, Audrey and I met Fern at the public library for one last time before the close of the school year. Since school was close enough to being over that we could celebrate, our minds were on summer vacation, but we still wanted to meet in the library one more time before we were officially sophomores.

As we walked, I imagined Miss Strayer in the same situation. Maybe she met her friends after school at the library? I made a mental note to ask her more about her time at St. Michael's.

We sat down at our usual table, after waving to the young librarian who knew all of our names by now. Fern plopped down in her chair with more than her usual enthusiasm. "So," she said. "Jenna asked me if I could go into the city with her this weekend. Just the two of us. We're going to some museums, and the park, and this fancy restaurant. I'm super excited."

"That's so awesome!" I exclaimed, remembering how distant Fern and Jenna had been when I first met them.

She nodded, a huge grin spreading across her face. "We haven't done something like that in years." I could tell from her expression how much it meant to her. "What are you guys doing this weekend? Celebrating?"

I shrugged. "Not much. I think we need some quiet, after all this."

Fern laughed. "I know, right? It's been a pretty crazy year."

Audrey's hands started moving. *You can say that again.*

We sunk back into silence, and started thinking. It had been a very crazy year. In the beginning of the year, I wondered if maybe I would end up back at home, learning from my mom's old high school textbooks, homeschooled again. But I was surprised to realize that I barely missed it at all. I think my mother would have been glad.

I thought about Audrey and her trees. I had eventually gotten used to it, and even read some of the books she had recommended. And I found that she was right. Our root systems were connected. More so than I ever thought before.

The thing about trees is that they are pretty much mirror images of themselves above and below the ground. As a tree grows upward and outward, its roots grow deeper and deeper, and the deeper they go, the more they intertwine, forming a stronger, more complex network.

Audrey and I were very different. There was no denying that. But our roots were deep.

epiloguE:

TWO GIRLS TUMBLE OUT of an old minivan. The sun is rising over the distant mountains, on the first day of a new school year. Rosemary Cooper, dressed in blue jeans and a polka-dotted t-shirt, hauls something out of the trunk of the car with a kitten tucked under her arm while her sister Audrey, in a light sweater, scoops up the reluctant cat who sits curled up on the passenger seat, asleep.

Their father grins as they walk together across a field, to a single, simple headstone. The girls smile as they place a handmade bouquet of wildflowers on the top of the stone. Audrey pulls something from her backpack. It is a small garden trowel, and a little bag of topsoil. Rosemary sets down the large bundle that she carries, unwrapping it to reveal a small, potted tree.

Somewhere in the background, *Let It Be* plays tinnily from the minivan.

The two girls lock eyes across the stone, and smile. Audrey sets down her bag and begins to dig a few feet behind the stone. Rosemary gently lifts the tree out of the little ceramic pot, letting the roots dangle in the air for a moment before lowering it into the hole that Audrey has dug. The two girls push the soil around the baby tree, while Benjamin the cat yowls in their father's arms. They laugh.

Audrey and Rosemary wipe their hands in the still-wet grass, looking up at the mountains behind their mother's grave, while their father, holding the squirming cat and the yowling kitten, smiles at them.

So, the girls' father says with a grin, *are you going to tell Mommy about the crazy year you had, or should I?*

Rosemary laughs. *There's too much to tell!*

Audrey looks at the newly-planted tree. *She knows.*

Rosemary tilts her head, deep in thought. *There was the beach with Fern, and the trip to the symphony orchestra with Miss Strayer.*

Audrey chimes in. *And my first piano recital and the time Benjamin escaped and we had to chase him all over the neighborhood!*

Their father laughs as the kitten chews on the cuff of his shirt. *And this is Beethoven, the newest member of the family.*

Rosemary laughs, watching the antics of the two cats, who roll around in the wet, green, late-summer grass.

Their father nods. After a brief silence, he glances at his watch, smiling at his daughters. *All right, we should probably get going. You girls ready for sophomore year?*

Rosemary and Audrey nod, sharing a look that says *I can't believe it.* They walk up to the tree, admiring their work one last time before saying goodbye to their mother. But it isn't really goodbye, and they know that.

As their father walks back to the minivan, Rosemary looks at Audrey, and her hands begin to flutter like leaves in the wind. Leaves on the top of a newly planted tree. *Are you ready?* she asks with a mischievous grin.

Audrey smiles and looks down, where under her feet, the roots of a new tree are beginning to spread. Her hands reach up to touch one of the thin, fragile leaves. After a moment, she turns and takes Rosemary's hand, pulling her to the car. With her free hand, she signs something to her sister, who smiles.

THE END

ELISE STANKUS

author's note

The first draft of my Author's Note was long and meandering, and it included several symbolic quotes and personal anecdotes. I eventually realized that if you made it this far, you are probably thoroughly sick of quotes and anecdotes, and so I changed my mind. As Rosemary would remind me: I don't have to torture you any further with my poetic tendencies. The best way to say something is to just say it.

So, thank you. Thank you for reading my book and making it yours. Thank you for accompanying Rosemary and Audrey through the first year of high school, and thank you for accompanying me through the process of writing and publishing. I believe in the enormous power of the written word, but a typed acknowledgment cannot express my gratitude to everyone who helped make this book a reality.

Firstly, I have to thank Megan H., who suggested I embark on the crazy, month-long journey that is NaNoWriMo - National Novel Writing Month - and without whom I would have never finished the first draft. This novel is the culmination of years of practice and hundreds of hours of writing, rewriting, and editing, and it wouldn't have happened without you.

To my family, who let me write when I should have been doing chores, who celebrated with me as I hit word count checkpoints, and who were my first readers. You made my job easier; I never had to think too hard about writing the happy family scenes because the perfect model was right in front of me. Thank you for everything.

To my brother, for keeping me company while I wrote, occupying yourself with whatever knickknacks happened to be on my floor as I furiously typed and persistently put off cleaning my workspace (a.k.a my room). Thank you for giving up your time for me and for this project. You were right - you deserve your own acknowledgement.

To the VVA graduating class of 2021, for encouraging me and making me laugh with such priceless phrases as "Future World-Famous Author" and "Miss Soon-To-Be-Published" and "Nerd In The Best Way Possible." Thank you for giving me the kind of wonderful high school experience I can only hope to have provided for my characters.

To my cousin Daniel Mulcahy, for agreeing to design and create the cover art, and for collaborating with me on all of the random design ideas I had along the way.

To Alicia Ribeiro, my friend and editor, for her exceptional advice and support.

To Mr. D., whose publishing advice probably saved me a couple of meltdowns and who is a pretty cool author role model.

To Mr. L., for introducing me to the Schrodinger's Cat idea and for encouraging me along the way.

To Mrs. S., for teaching about tree communications on the day I began writing this book, for planting in my mind the seed of a story (pun intended). You truly changed the trajectory of this novel for the better.

To Peter Wohlleben, whose groundbreaking and captivating studies of forests led to my fascination with trees.

To Madeleine L'Engle, Joan Bauer, John Green, C.S. Lewis, Lois Lowry, Cynthia Kadohata, Sharon Creech, Jerry Spinelli, Neil Gaiman, Antoine de Saint Exupéry, GennaRose Nethercott, Jeanne Birdsall, Regina Doman, and all the other writers whose works enchanted me so much that I made it my personal mission to someday write something as influential to others as their works had been to me.

Finally, I thank God, because without Him, I would not be here at all, much less here AND publishing a novel at eighteen. He has blessed me without measure through the people mentioned above, and I am eternally grateful.

See you in the next book!

about the author

Elise Stankus lives in New Jersey with her parents, younger brother, and rabbit. When she is not writing, she enjoys playing various musical instruments, reading all sorts of books, and exploring the world by bike. Elise currently attends college in the Philadelphia area, where she is pursuing an English degree.

ELISE STANKUS

.

IF WE FALL IN THE FOREST

CPSIA information can be obtained
at www.ICGtesting.com
Printed in the USA
BVHW032159251021
619907BV00005B/39

9 781006 415265